I0673227

My Journey Home

Based on a True Story

Written by Lucie Grimm

1

It was a beautiful, bright, sunny, late summer day like any other in my hometown of Teplice in 1984. My kindergarten school was a one-story, one-room brick building, nestled against the gentle hills of thick, fragrant forest that gently cupped the city. As I exited the doors of my classroom for the last time this year, I found a sea of talkative parental faces waiting just outside. Among them was my beautiful mother, her short blonde hair glistening in the afternoon sun. She was wearing a sea-green top and a matching skirt that showed off her slim, curvy figure. She stood there smiling, with her arms outstretched to greet me. I ran to hug her. There was something about my mother's beaming smile. It was perfectly proportioned to her round face and yet it was huge. When she was happy, you could see all her teeth, top and bottom, yet it wasn't too much. She was a nurse by trade, but her years in cosmetology reflected on her put-together appearance every day. Her warm arms, strong and bare from the elbow down, greeted me. As she took me by the hand, we began the short, somewhat downhill walk to my grandmother's house along the uneven cobble streets of our neighborhood. My mother greeted neighbors she knew as we passed by, but I only recognized a few faces, focusing my attention on not tripping on the cobblestone. As we took our final turn, I saw my grandparent's five-story villa. It was made of large stone, and the years had created a dark-grey sheen over the rock, only avoiding the large white windows evenly distributed on each level. Almost all the color had gone from the panes and roof. The only things livening it up were the numerous bright-colored flowers that grew beneath it in a small, flat garden that all the tenants shared but mainly my grandmother and one other older woman tended to. There was a small garage that only one car fit into and a shared basement. My grandmother lived on the fifth floor. There were no elevators, so as people approached the front door to her flat, they were usually slowing down or gasping for air. I would always run the cold stone stairs and be the first one there.

Today, as we approached the building, I saw our tan Saab 900 parked along the curb right in front of the heavy wooden gate to the little garage. My father, lean and fit, stood assertively next to it, talking to my grandfather, my uncle, and two men I did not recognize. They all stood circling the car, opening and closing doors as if they were inspecting something. As we approached, I wanted to release my mother's soft grip on my hand and greet my father, but she held me fast. We were almost at the squeaky iron entry gate when my grandmother came walking through the main door of the building. She had a light summer dress that resembled a bone-white, linen Mumu, falling past her bosom and hiding her bulging belly. The sun caught her brownish red hair and gave life to her round, squishy face. Accompanying her was her bulky handheld purse. She smiled and waved to me as she closed the door behind her and joined my mother and me as we proceeded to walk past her building. I suddenly knew where we were going—the ice cream shop. It sat behind the villa my grandmother occupied. The city had not repainted the buildings in years and the wear of snow and sleet had caused all the buildings in the area to take on a dark-grey and, in some cases, black color that made them all look the same. But if you were the observant type, you would find intricate patterns carved in the stone that made each of the buildings unique and quite beautiful. We rounded the street corner and entered the small courtyard to the ice cream shop. It was just a little covered stand, big enough to house two people, right on the inside of the villa's garden fence, but it had the best Italian ice cream around. I ordered vanilla and strawberry, finding it hard to stand still until that creamy sweet mixture was touching my lips. The man over the counter handed me a two-scoop cone as big as my forearm and proceeded to tend to my mother and grandmother. I looked around the perfectly manicured garden and took a seat at one of the five closest iron bistro sets I could find, proceeding to indulge in my first scoop of ice cream. Vanilla.

Life seemed perfect. The afternoon sun shone brightly, everyone was happy and friendly, the multitude of flowers were in full bloom, colorful birds sang their songs, yellow and blue butterflies fluttered, and the bees buzzed their work away. Little did I know that this would be the last week that would feel this way for years to come. As my mother sat next to me, my grandmother started talking in a very serious tone. I was too young to grasp the concept of our situation or the words my grandmother used. Words like *communist, Russia, invasion, take over, emigration.* She talked of uncertain times and going to a place called America, but I didn't understand or pay much attention. These were not uncertain times; everything was wonderful. I didn't understand it, so I stopped listening. Here and there I overheard my grandmother asking questions like "What are you going to do?" "Where will you go?" But they seemed like silly questions and my attention was on the pretty blue and black butterfly that was circling around me as if it beckoned me to play.

When we returned to my grandma's villa, the men were all gone and the small tan car sat in silent stillness along the abandoned curb. We entered through the squeaky iron gate and walked up the three steps to the main door. My mother unlocked it, and we entered a cold, concrete stairwell with winding stairs all the way to the top. We began climbing. The building was made up of five flats, one on each level. Along the stairwell, we would pass double entry doors to each flat, surrounded by potted plants, some dead and some vivid green with life, and shoe racks, with nothing but old and heavily broken in men's, women's, and, in a couple of cases, children's shoes. As I approached the fifth floor, the scenery became familiar—two tall green plants in their blue and white containers sitting by the large staircase window that gave light to the cold hall. And then the final ten steps brought me to Grandma's double, glass-pane front door. There was no shoe rack there; it was perfectly clean and groomed, with just a front-door, straw-like mat to greet you. The door was locked, and my mother and grandmother were both quite far behind. I could hear them talking, out of breath and pushing to make it the final stretch. I didn't want to wait. I rang the bell and listened to the melodic chimes echo inside. My grandfather opened the right side of the door, and I ran into his arms to greet him. He was like a teddy bear—warm, soft, and round, smelling like cookies and aftershave. It was my favorite smell. He was a jolly man with bushy eyebrows, a big nose, full cheeks, and small, beady eyes. He laughed his jolly laugh as he helped me get my shoes off and then led me into the all-wood dining room, where my father sat over a cup of hot coffee and delicious sweet deserts that my grandmother had made the day prior. The room had hardwood floors that creaked slightly under the weight of each step from years of traffic. There was a four-foot-high china cabinet running along the length of the wall closest to the hall, that my grandmother had custom made for the room, and a large formal dining table made of polished cherry wood that seated six or more when stretched out. I greeted my father and sat in the chair nearest him. It felt like I had interrupted a previous conversation as they fell silent all of a sudden, until my father asked me how school had been. Nothing exciting.

My father was a handsome young man. Slender and fit from years of service in the air force. His eyes were the same blue as the skies he flew in. He had thinning light-brown hair that my mother recently cut short. His nose was thin and long like mine, and he had a smile that sparked like diamonds. Although he had had them fixed years ago, his ears were still his most prominent feature, but he would rather you not mention them at all. I was told many times I was the spitting image of my father, but, personally, I just didn't see it.

My grandmother served an early dinner in that same room only moments later. She proudly served it on her blue Danube china, a very expensive china set that was made only a short drive away. It was white with blue flowers printed in an intricate pattern around the very edge of it. She had the entire collection—plates, bowls, cups, saucers, and coffee and tea sets, everything. I used to admire it in her china cabinet when it wasn't in use. We had a feast that night. Steaming garlic soup with toasted croutons, followed by dumplings with green sauerkraut and tender roast pig. It was absolutely scrumptious. After everyone had their fill, I helped clear the table, and Grandma served coffee and tea alongside her fresh-baked fruit tart. I was too full to even consider desert, but when my eyes fell on the tart with its sugar-crumb topping, I at least had to have a sliver. It melted in my mouth. I could taste tart cherries and sweet raspberries, and the sugar-crumb topping brought it all together. My mother poured me some Earl Grey tea and they began their discussions. I wasn't interested, but there was nothing else left for me to do but sit and listen.

My normally quiet grandfather began the discussion, asking if my parents had truly thought it through.

My father answered first. "We figure that if we can get into Austria, we can get asylum there and request a visa into America. My coworker knows a guy who wants to leave, too. I think if we go as a group, we may have a better chance."

"Peter and Lenka want to go, too, so we would have someone to travel with until we get there," said my mother.

Peter was my mother's older brother and Lenka was his wife of two years. They had a daughter named Petra, who was almost one year old.

"But no one is allowed out of Czechoslovakia. How are you going to get past the boarders?" asked Grandma.

"It's not that you are not allowed. You have to ask the government for permission and follow their protocol," my father replied, "and we got the permission."

"What do you mean?" my grandmother pressed on.

"We are a socialist country. You can travel through any other socialist countries without question. It's the capitalist countries we are not allowed in," he explained. My grandmother nodded as if she had heard this before. "Yugoslavia is both, so we asked for permission to go there for vacation and got it," he continued. "Eva is setting up the designated bank account they require and transferring funds this week. Once we do, they will issue our gas vouchers."

"We have to travel through socialist countries so we have to go all the way around by going through Hungary into Yugoslavia and crossing the border there," my mother clarified.

"I don't like it. This is very risky. Let's say you make it. What then? What will you do? Where will you go?" My grandmother began to get distraught and was holding back her tears. "When will I see you again and my little Lucie?" she asked as she wiped her face with her handkerchief, which seemed to somehow be with her always. "What if they find out we knew about it? They could lock us up, too," she added.

I suddenly realized something big was going on, but no one took the time to fill me in. What was my part in all this? I felt confused and overwhelmed with information I didn't understand. I decided to get up and go play in the other room. There was nothing on TV at this hour, so I went into my grandmother's kitchen and into the pantry. I knew it was an odd place to disappear to, but there was something about this room that gave me a sense of peace. It had tall glass doors to a tiny outside patio that Grandma had filled with potted plants she obviously forgot about every so often as they were frail and dry. The small room itself had everything from sewing supplies to canned foods, but mainly a large fabric bag, almost bigger than me, filled with walnuts from her garden at her weekend house in the country. The smell was earthy and calming. I sat in the corner on a small wooden footstool and tried to make sense of what was going on and how I felt. It was all a jumble and I found myself staring out the window, then scanning all the things in that pantry, inspecting the spots where the linoleum was peeling from the floor, and feeling confused. After what seemed like only a few minutes, my mother found me and walked me to the hallway leading to the front door. My father had our jackets and shoes all ready. We were leaving. We all said our good-byes; the hugs seemed oddly longer, and the kisses that met my cheeks were wet and extra hard. I smiled and said good-bye, but I was still lost in my own head.

I sat in the backseat of our little Saab as we made the fifteen-minute drive home, waiting for my parents to say something, anything, but they were quiet. Not even the radio kept us company on that ride home.

2

We lived in a decent part of town, in a villa similar to my grandparents', but ours wasn't cradled in a beautiful garden. In fact, it had somewhat of a cold, concrete feel. There was a fairly long concrete bridge you had to cross to get to the front door; the drop around the bridge was deadly and scary, with nothing but concrete and scattered trash below. Unlike my grandparent's villa, ours had an elevator. It scared me to take it, however, as it was old and rickety, so I always tried to take the cement stairs. We lived on the fourth floor. The flat was nice and homey but not nearly as large or high class as my grandparent's flat. It emptied into a wide hallway, which housed a couple of cabinets, our shoe racks, and a bathroom. The floors were linoleum throughout, and the walls within the unit were thin and seemed temporary. To the right were the living room, dining room, and kitchen, and to the left was the bedroom I shared with my parents. It was a large, decently lit bedroom. They had their bed on one side, next to the built-in closet. I had mine on the other by the door. At the foot of my bed was a tall wooden cabinet that housed all my toys.

I woke up the next morning to chaos. My mother was already up. She had not bothered to do her hair or makeup yet and was running about the apartment, collecting random objects and placing them into cardboard boxes that were lined up by the front door. As I walked past the hallway to make my way to breakfast, I saw several of these boxes already half full. Some had clothes, other had pots and pans, and still others had canned foods and powder mixes. I wasn't sure what they were for, but my tired mind could only accept their presence at this moment and move on.

I entered the kitchen. It was all white with orange Formica cabinets. Not a cabinet choice I would make today, but at the time, it seemed appropriate, and its brightness brought on a feeling of pure happiness when you entered. My mother had made soft-boiled eggs, my favorite. I don't know if I liked the flavor as much as the action of carefully sitting each egg in a beautifully decorated ceramic egg holder that almost put it on a pedestal, as if it were royalty. She made me Earl Grey tea and there were a few slices of dense rye bread and butter. After she placed the food in front of me and was satisfied that I had everything I needed, she proceeded to bustle about again. I finished my breakfast slowly and in peace, finishing two soft-boiled eggs and one slice of buttered bread, and cleared the table. She seemed awfully busy this morning, so I put away the uneaten food and went to my room to get dressed. She was going through the closet, pulling out random bits of clothing, inspecting them closely and tossing them in various piles on the bed.

"I'm going to go play with Radek," I said.

Without pausing to look at me, she said, "Okay, just be careful and don't wander off."

My best friend Radek lived on the third floor just below us. He was a boy I had known since I was born. His parents were heavy smokers, and his appearance sometimes looked gaunt and sickly, but he was a kind person and a good friend. He was the same age as I was, and it seemed as though we were the only kids in that building and the buildings around it.

I put on my black slip-on shoes and left the chaos of the morning. I went down the cold cement stairs one level to Radek's flat and rang the doorbell. Within moments, he answered it. His dark hair was still wet but perfectly combed to one side, and his small face seemed to light up, emphasizing the dimples in his round cheeks, when he saw me. He disappeared for a split moment to grab his shoes and then joined me in the hall. We ran down the remaining flights of stairs and out the heavy-glassed front doors. The warm morning sun burst upon us, blinding us, but that didn't stop us. We happily ran across the cement bridge and to the right of the building. As we were approaching our regular hangout, I noticed my father on the curb alongside our parked car. I stopped and curiously started walking toward him, Radek at my heels. As I got closer, I realized that there was a tall, thin policeman with him. I slowed down in caution, but continued walking. The policeman handed my father a small piece of paper and shook his hand before parting. My father saw me and smiled, but I could tell from the expression on his face that it was not a happy smile, more like a polite one. As I looked past him to our car, I noticed there was shattered glass on the street around it. Our car had been broken into. As I glanced in the car through the broken passenger's window, I saw nothing but a handful of colored wires sticking out of the center console where the radio once lived. The stereo and all our cassettes were gone!

"At least that is all they took," my father said, patting me on the shoulder.

All they took?!? They took my favorite cassette tapes! I was angry and sad, but the pressure of my father's hand on my shoulder reassured me of something I didn't understand, and I let it go.

"Go play, Lucie. We are going to go to my mom's house for the weekend. So we will leave in a few hours," he said.

"Can Radek come?" I asked, not even knowing if he could.

"Not this time, Sweetie. Maybe some other time," he replied.

I nodded understandingly and turned to leave. Radek took me by the hand, and we started walking, our cupped hands swaying with each step. I only glanced at my father once and only over my shoulder, to see him rubbing his forehead and shaking his head in despair. I could tell he was upset, and it made me sad that I couldn't comfort him and make it better.

To the right side of the villa was a little patch of cement ruins. There must have been another building here at one point in time, but what it had been I could only guess. There was a cement floor with rebar sticking out on one side, no more than the size of a large playhouse, followed by a large berry bush, lush green with tricolored berries the birds fed on, and then a one-and-a-half-story drop to a pile of cement rubble and sharp, jagged rocks among which you were bound to find coins, broken bottles, and other things people had uncaringly discarded there. Our hangout was on that top part of the remaining cement, although my mother didn't like us hanging here, as a couple of years back, I took a fall here. I took a wrong step and fell between the protruding rebar onto the rocks below, ending up in the hospital with bruises, scrapes, and lots of pain, but luckily, nothing was broken. I'd been extra careful ever since.

Radek and I were best friends, but we never really went anywhere together. This was it, our spot. We talked here, played house here; it was our place away from the rest of the world.

Today, I had to talk to him about it. No one else would talk to me. I told him about the men inspecting the car and the funny words I'd been hearing from my family, and about the packing and the weird behavior. He wasn't able to clarify much for me, but he did say he heard his parents talking about the Russians trying to take over our country and that they were provoking war. But what had that got to do with us? I hadn't seen any Russians here. He tried to comfort me and tell me it was all going to be okay, but somehow, I wasn't convinced.

Before I knew it, my mother was serving lunch and then my dad started packing up the car with the boxes my mother had been preparing all day. He had fixed the passenger window with tape and cardboard for the drive. I grabbed my favorite toy, a brick-red rabbit almost as big as me, with long limbs and long ears that dangled as he moved. I had never bothered to name him, but he was a toy I dragged with me everywhere. I had dressed him in tropical shorts and a T-shirt for the trip, and we were off.

3

My father's parents lived in the country about an hour's ride away, in a place called Oldrichov. It was a beautiful drive past a peaceful lake I liked visiting. The lake had black sand, which I later learned was a result of the coal that was mined from its base. Beautiful white swans had made it their home, and we would go out there to feed them and swim in the lake during the heat of the summer. A thin forest of pine lined the back of the lake, and meadows of flowers and grass held it in place.

My father's parents were of simpler breed. Their two-story house sat on a large parcel of land that they had cultivated to grow everything they needed to put food on their table. They grew potatoes, cucumbers, strawberries, turnips, lettuce, tomatoes, and a handful of fruits. They also had a pig and about fifteen rabbits that they raised for food. It was a "simpler" way of living. Their neighbors raised cows and chickens, and they traded their vegetables or meat for the neighbors' eggs and milk. I liked coming here. My grandmother, Mirka, would make us carbonated drinks and we would sit on her two-person metal swing at the back of the house and watch the world go by. I mainly liked coming here to feed the rabbits. Their fuzzy ears and soft fur were like a magnet to me. I would pull up some lettuce and turnips from the rich earth and take each rabbit out of his cage. I would sit on the grass in front of their enclosures and hand-feed each little furry ball of life. It was a comforting pastime.

This time, as we pulled up to the house, Grandpa, in his dirty blue overalls and white, wiry chest hair sticking through the top, opened the gate for us so we could pull into the gravel drive. He smiled, revealing only a couple of his remaining teeth, as we passed. He was a sweet man with a good heart and a hard worker, but his appearance showed his lack of care for himself. He had a thick head of curly black hair that never seemed to need combing, he only possessed a handful of teeth, he never wore a shirt, and he smelled of sweat and lived in his overalls whenever he could. He was my father's stepdad, but my father treated him as if he had watched over him his whole life. He was Slovak and spoke a different dialect than the rest of my family, and I found it hard to understand him a lot of the time, but I loved him.

Grandma had prepared soup and rabbit in a hardy cream sauce with some fluffy bread dumplings for lunch. She was a heavyset woman with squishy cheeks and squishy arms. She had thin, light-blonde, curly hair that tickled her ears and fell just past the base of her head.

After eating our fill, I went outside to play in the garden while my parents unloaded the car. Grandpa inspected the broken window, Grandma was helping my mother put our things in the bedroom, and I was free to frolic in the tall summer grass. I walked the rows of ripening potatoes and radishes that were so perfectly separated into aisles. The strawberries were ripe, and I picked a handful to munch on as I passed. They were small but extra sweet. Then I got to the rows of lettuces and turnips. I knelt down next to the flowering lettuce and started pulling off the dark, green leaves from the outer edge of the ball, just like Grandma had taught me, leaving the main part of the vegetable for us to eat later. Then the turnips. They were too young to pick still, so I pulled off some of the jagged leaves from its crown. Once I had a decent handful, I made my way to the wooden rabbit cages that were stacked on top of each other against the back wall of the house. I began my ritual. One by one, I took a rabbit out of his cage and placed him in my lap. I gave him a leaf to munch on and he, in exchange, held still while I rubbed his strong, long ears and petted his soft, deep fur. When he refused to eat any more, I placed him back and moved to the next one. It kept me busy for a couple of hours but never felt like it was really that long. They had rabbits of many colors—all white, black, brown, grey, and various spotted combinations. Looking back now, I wondered how I could have been so naïve to not associate the rabbits I fed with the ones that ended up on the dinner table.

When I emerged from the yard, I found my father cutting into the back leather seat of our Saab. Using a razor blade, he was carefully cutting along the edge of the tan stitching that housed the cushion I usually sat on. Grandpa had magically fixed the broken passenger window and was carefully putting the door panel back in place.

"What are you doing, Daddy?" I inquired, hoping he would give me something to do.

"I'm trying to figure something out here. Why don't you see if your mother needs any help in the house?" he answered.

I hesitated for only a moment and then did as I was told. I walked into the house, removed my shoes at the door, and entered the small, dark kitchen, where my grandmother was washing the dishes. I asked her if she needed any help. She smiled and said, "No, my dear, but thank you. Why don't you see if your mother needs anything? She is upstairs in the bedroom."

I walked up the wooden staircase to the room where my mother was. She seemed sad and stressed. She was folding clothing into perfect squares. When she saw me, she stopped and smiled a toothless smile, and her sadness seemed to fade.

"Do you need any help?" I asked.

"Sure," she said. "Why don't you help me put all these folded items into a laundry basket? We are going to take them down to your father."

I felt like I had an important mission all of a sudden. I ran down the hall to grab the laundry basket my grandmother kept in the closet with the linens and returned with great concentration, carefully stacking the clothing into the basket. Once it was full and perfectly organized. I dragged the basket to the top of the stairs. My mother picked it up, and together, we walked it to the car. The afternoon sun was already starting to orange, and the men were hard at work. The backseat of the car was completely disassembled. The stuffing was completely removed, leaving the shell of the seat and the springs within it. The same was done to the part of the seat that you lean on. My mother placed the laundry basket full of clothing next to the car and proceeded to move the boxes we had brought closer to that same general area. My father then started taking one item out of the box at a time and puzzle-pieced it into the exposed seat.

He took the heavy-duty pressure cooker first. He filled it with odds and ends from the boxes until it was full and then pieced it into the center cushion underneath the springs, careful not to cut himself on the springs. Next came the set of three pots that fit nicely into each other. But my dad took them apart and placed kitchen towels between each layer and then shook the whole thing.

"That should be good," said my mother in response.

My father proceeded to find a place in the cushions to fit this set of pots. It was obvious he was trying to keep them from making noise, but why? And why was he putting our stuff in the seats? I didn't question what they were doing out loud, but in my head, I was overwhelmed with questions. My father would stick a shirt here, a frying pan there, canned food item here, a dry food mixture there. It went on and on like that. I felt useless to help, so after observing for a while, I went inside. Grandma was making little open-faced sandwiches for dinner. She asked me if I wanted to help. I shrugged as I accepted the packages of sliced ham and cheese that I was to distribute on the butter-smeared rye bread already laid out on the table. I quietly completed my task and sat down. I fell silent. My mind was going a million miles an hour. I tried to make sense of what was going on but I was too afraid to ask. I sat there, still, staring into the floorboards as if it would bring some clarity to the situation.

"Are you okay Lucie?" my grandmother whispered.

I didn't have the energy to look at her or answer her. She must have walked away because the next thing I knew, my father was petting my head.

"Thank you for making the sandwiches. They look very good."
I haphazardly smiled without looking up. "Will you have one
with me?" he asked.

I slowly nodded, numb inside. But I didn't want to disappoint
him, so I picked up a sandwich and began taking small bites. It
was full of bright, mouthwatering flavor and made me feel
better. As I finally looked around, I found myself surrounded
by everyone at the table. They were all eating and drinking,
smiling and satisfied at their hard day's work. The atmosphere
seemed to be cheerful and brought me out of my daze. When
we finished eating, we played a game of dice. There was no
talk of things I couldn't grasp or discussions of what lie ahead
or what had transpired that day. We laughed, ate and merrily
played the hours away. Before I knew it, it was past my
bedtime.

4

The next day, my grandmother took me to the lake. She said she had some stale bread she didn't want to throw out and asked if I would go with her to feed the swans. I was so excited I barely noticed my parents getting into the same tasks as they did the day before.

The lake was extra pretty today. The late morning sun was bright but not blinding, the water was nearly still as glass only rippling where the majestic white swans passed through it. It was deep and, even though the sand was pitch black, the water was perfectly clear, allowing you to see the bottom without trying. There was no one around. Today, it was our playground. She handed me a bag of bread, and we approached the water's edge, throwing a few small chunks in the water. It must have been like ringing the dinner bell. The swans that were slowly and majestically swimming along were now swimming quickly and with purpose toward us. One, two, four, six. Nine swans in total made their way toward the bread we had thrown. They were as big as me, tall and majestic and white as snow with orange beaks like the setting sun. I was in awe and in fear at the same time. I was afraid they would attack me for the bag I held, but my grandmother stood her ground. Calmly taking out a handful of stale bread bits and scattering them along the crystal-clear water line. Within seconds, the swans began picking the bread off the surface with grace and poise yet great speed. They made me smile with sweet bliss. I followed my grandmother's lead and tossed a handful of bread bits in front of me. As the swans recognized that there was plenty coming their way, they slowed down and ate more calmly. My grandmother must have had experience with this because she then took another handful of bread bits, but this time, she did not throw them. She kept them in her hand as she extended her squishy arm toward them and allowed two of the swans to eat from it. She prompted me to touch them. I hesitated for a moment before extending my hand to touch their white, clean feathers. They were soft but strong. I smiled and looked at my grandmother with pride. She then put some bits in my little hand and held it out for the swans to feed. I was nervous doing this, but her sturdy hand under mine reassured my safety.

We spent the day there. Grandma had packed us a sandwich lunch and had brought towels and my swimsuit. We made sand castles out of the sparkling black sand, walked the beach, skipped stones, swam the crystal-clear waters and fed the majestic birds. It was a perfect day.

Around mid-afternoon, we started our short walk back to the house. Grandma bought me an ice-cream cone along the way from a local vendor and we happily strolled along past all her neighbors. We didn't say much to each other, but it didn't feel like we had to. I was happy. When we walked through the metal gate to the property, it was quiet. The car, yet again, sat in quiet stillness, fully intact as if nothing had ever happened to it. There were no more boxes or tools scattered along the drive.

We made our way inside. Mother was in the kitchen making food, which I knew was hot because the steam the rose from it carried a sweet scent to my nose. Grandpa, still in overalls and no shirt, was listening to the radio, and my father's footsteps could be heard shuffling upstairs. I was told to wash up and change, as dinner was ready. There was an unsettling peace in the surroundings, but as Grandma nudged me to walk upstairs, I gave in to my instructions. I found my father neatly folding his unused clothes and piling other random personal items into his bag that sat on the bed. His hair was wet and he smelled of soap. He seemed to be lost in thought as I entered the room.

"Hi, Daddy!"

"Hi, Lucie. Did you have fun at the lake?"

I nodded. "Good. Why don't you go wash up? Mom has food about ready so we will go down and eat. It was a busy day here, and we didn't have time to eat lunch."

"Okay." I grabbed myself my sweatpants and a clean shirt from the luggage next to the door and made my way to the small bathroom.

When I returned downstairs, everyone was already sitting at the small kitchen table, talking happily. The smell of food filled the room, as my mother served everyone individually. She had made a tomato sauce over tender beef strips and bread dumplings. It was a little late to be serving food of this size, but no one seemed to object and dug in with great satisfaction. The table fell silent.

5

After having breakfast the next morning, my mother and I loaded the car with our luggage, and I carefully place my brick-red rabbit in the backseat and buckled him in. There was a lot less stuff going home with us. No more boxes, and two of the suitcases we had brought were empty and light. We said our good-byes and left. I watched the countryside pass us by as I tried to put together the pieces of the past few days. Nothing made sense to me; I was frustrated and fell into a quiet fog. My attention fell to the seats I sat on. There was new stitching around the seams of the seat. It wasn't obvious but definitely there. The seats felt harder than usual and I found myself shifting to settle into a comfortable spot. My parents were pretty quiet throughout the drive, only speaking to discuss stopping or changing the radio station. After an hour, the scenery began to change to the familiar city we lived in, but we were not going home. We were making our way toward Grandma's villa. I was tired from the drive and anxious to get home, but it seemed home would have to wait. As we pulled up, I noticed Uncle Peter's car parked on the otherwise abandoned curb.

Dad parked our car behind Uncle Peter's, and we made our way to the fifth floor. Arriving first, I rang the bell. My smiling grandpa greeted me. He was excited to see me and gave me a big bear hug, filling my nose with the familiar smell of cookies and cologne I had come to know. He helped me get my shoes off as my parents entered through the door. I ran into the kitchen to look for my grandmother. She wasn't there. So I ran back through the hall into the dining room. I found her setting out plates in front of each chair of the cherry wood table, and Lenka was helping her with the silverware. Uncle Peter sat at the end of the table, slumped over, as he usually did, sipping on a cup of coffee. I gave them all hugs in greeting. We had obviously stopped by to eat. It was rare to have Uncle Peter and Lenka there for lunch, so I was excited to see them.

Uncle Peter had the same nose, lips, and smile as my mother, It was the only traits they shared. When either of them smiled, they lit up the room with their pearly whites. Uncle Peter was tall and big boned, giving the impression of a husky, big man, although he was fairly fit. Lenka was significantly shorter, with thin black hair cut so short in stuck straight up in places like a boy's. Unlike Uncle Peter, she had almost no lips and even though she was pleasant looking, I never thought of her as beautiful but she was always nice to me.

As the family made their way into the dining room, Grandma disappeared into the kitchen to prepare lunch. After the round of hellos and smiles, my mother disappeared into the kitchen, too. She came back moments later empty handed and joined the group. When we had all taken our seats at the table, Grandma appeared with her two-tier, wooden dining trolley. On the top tier was a white porcelain serving dish full of freshly made soup, which she began to ladle into each person's bowl. Each person waited till everyone had their serving before they began to eat. It was a common courtesy that everyone was accustomed to.

There was no quiet at the table today. Everyone was talking. Uncle Peter was sharing his stories about work, and mother offered her opinions to dilemmas and situations. I was catching phrases here and there, but the topics really disinterested me. I was enjoying the company and trying to fit in, but spending most of my time enjoying Grandma's delicious tripe soup. Grandma was the first to finish her portion, as usual, as she tried to eat elegantly but quickly so that she could prepare the next segment of the meal. I often thought she should get a server or a butler to help her. She disappeared with the trolley and empty serving bowl. I was done, too, and got up to help.

When I got into the kitchen, she smiled at me as if she had a secret.

"I made your favorite today. It took me all morning, but I think they turned out perfect," she said as she opened the silver steam pot to reveal a pile of round, off-white, fluffy dumplings.

"Fruit-filled dumplings!" I screeched. "What kind are they?"

"I ran out of blueberries half way through, so there are blueberry and the rest are apricot. Why don't you grab the cheese from the refrigerator, I already have the butter melting, and then go grab everyone's plate. It will be easier to prepare them all here."

I happily obliged. I grabbed the wedge of cheese and quickly handed it to my grandmother to grate before running out of the room to grab the plates. I found I could only carry four at a time. They were too heavy and I was afraid of dropping them.

Mother offered to help, but I told her I could do it. When I was almost out of the room, I heard Uncle Peter say, "Have you told her?" I paused in my tracks. What did he mean? Was he referring to me? I was torn, do I go back and listen or would that be too obvious? I quickly walked the plates into the kitchen. After Grandma took them, I ran back into the dining room, hoping to catch the answer to the previous question, hoping that I would learn what the question had meant. No such luck. As I collected the remaining plates, Uncle Peter was asking my father about a rumbling sound his car was making, hoping he could get some insight into what it was and how to fix it. I missed my chance.

When I got back into the kitchen with the remaining plates, Grandma had already prepared a small wooden stool for me by the counter. She took the remaining plates from me and I carefully stood up on the stool. She placed four plates, side by side, in front of me.

"The blueberry dumplings are on the right and the apricots are on the left. Give everyone two of each," she said as she placed the silver steaming pot on the counter to my right.

I placed two of each type of dumpling on the pretty blue and white china using a slotted wooden spoon, putting them perfectly in the middle. As I did so, my grandmother cut into the top of each dumpling with a short little knife, causing steam to bellow out at us. The cut was only big enough to expose the inside fruit to the toppings that came next.

"Be careful, the butter is hot." She handed me a silver tablespoon. I ladled one tablespoon of melted butter over the top of each dumpling, and Grandma followed it by putting a handful of grated cheese over the four dumplings. My mouth instantly began to water; I couldn't wait to dig in. Then came the sour cream and the white powdered sugar. Finally, one more final drizzle of melted butter. It honestly looked like a white mound of mush, but the taste was intoxicating. We carefully put each finished plate on the trolley, two on the top tier and two on the bottom. As Grandma prepared the remaining plates, my job was to take the trolley into the dining room. Once there, mother helped me place a plate in front of the first four people so that I could take the trolley to get the rest.

Within moments, everyone was served, and I was sitting at the table. Some people complained it was too big of a portion, others said the dish looked great. Everyone fiddled with their drinks, but this time, for me, table etiquette went out the window. I wasn't waiting for anyone. I dug into the dumpling mush. The steam and smell of hot blueberries bellowed out at me. My mouth instantly watered, preparing itself for the tastes I was about to experience. My first bite filled me with joy, the second filled me with warmth, and the rest put me into my own little bubble. I switched from blueberry to apricot to blueberry again and before I knew it, my plate was empty and my belly about to pop with four dumplings comfortably nestled in my tummy. I couldn't move, didn't want to either. I was happy. It seemed like everyone was taking a pause following their filling lunch. After a few moments, Lenka and my mother helped clear the table of all the dishes and uneaten portions and brought back tea and coffee in gold-painted porcelain serving kettles. Then the conversations began. It started with my grandpa.

"Have you all really thought this through? What about your things? Your flats?" he said with a sudden tone of concern.

My ears perked up. I wanted to know what was going on. I looked from my grandpa to my mother then my father. I saw my mother indicate to me with a glance as if to remind my grandfather that I was there.

"We packed most of the items we need and worked them into the car," said my father. "As long as no one searches it in great detail, we should be fine."

So that is what he was doing. So we are going somewhere. Why won't anyone fill me in? Why can't they tell me what is going on?

"About that...," Uncle Peter interrupted." We have had a change of situation and won't be able to go with you."

My mother suddenly looked scared. "What do you mean? This has been planned!" She searched Lenka's guilty face and then her brother's.

"Lenka is pregnant with another child," he said. My grandmother shrieked with excitement, but everyone else fell silent. "It's just too risky and with the one baby we have and now a second on the way, we are not sure it is the best timing for us."

There was silence, as everyone took time to absorb this new information.

"Okay. We understand," said my father quietly. He stared at his coffee as he said it. He must have realized his body language and looked up at Uncle Peter quickly. "Congratulations, you guys. I'm really happy for you."

"Maybe you guys should reconsider going. Stay here. We can live through it, it will all be okay," said Grandma.

"We have already given our resignations and made arrangements. It's the better option for us,", my father replied. "We still have the family we are meeting up within Hungary or Split who are to go with us. We will be okay."

So Split is where we are going? But why? Am I going, too? Then the realization hit me. What if I'm not going with them? Maybe that is why they haven't told me anything. I began to get scared.

"Lucie is out of school and we have informed only those that need to know. We told everyone else, neighbors and our jobs and friends a different story to make this plausible. Everything is in place," he said, "The family we are to meet up with are also Czech, and they have two children Lucie's age."

Oh thank God! I am going. Of course, I'm going. They wouldn't leave me behind.

My mother chimed in, "Since you are not going, Peter, maybe you could help us move our furniture out. We have sold most of it, but there are a few things maybe you and Mom could take until I can find a way to get them once we are settled in."

"I can swing by tomorrow," he replied.

She nodded in response. The table suddenly fell silent and uncomfortable. I felt the tension in the room, or maybe it was my full stomach pushing on my innards, but either way, I had some new knowledge. My grandparents didn't seem to be too happy about it, and it seemed we were going with Uncle Peter, but now we are going alone. I know Split. We used to vacation there every so often. It was warm and sunny and the beaches were beautiful with warm clear water. I was excited to go back there. Who was this other family we were meeting? Father said they had two children my age. I wonder if they will like me.

"We should probably get home," my father said. "We still have a lot to take care of today."

With that statement, everyone seemed to get up and start gathering their belongings. The good-byes were even worse than last time. The hugs seemed to last forever and seemed sad. Grandma smothered me with wet kisses, her eyes tearing, and then swooped me up for just one more bone-breaking hug. Everyone seemed to be teary eyed. I didn't know what to do. I place my hand on my grandma's freckled bare arm and said, "It's okay. We will be back soon." Among her handkerchief and tears, she laughed and nodded.

We descended the stone staircase to the car and headed home.

The afternoon was spent in confusion. People I didn't know were stopping by the house and leaving with our things— dining table and chairs, kitchen appliances, and other things. Mother was unpacking then packing again. Father was counting money, then sorting through things in the closets and spending a lot of time on the phone.

That evening, during dinner, my parents sat me down.

"Sweetie, I know you are too young to understand, but we feel we should explain," my mother said. "We are going on a trip. A long trip."

"But we are coming back, right?" I asked.

"Maybe one day, but never to this house," said my father.

"But why?" I cried.

"It's complicated, honey. There are some bad people coming into our cities and they are doing bad things. We want to get away so they don't hurt us," explained my mother.

"Are Grandma and Grandpa coming?"

"No, dear. They are going to stay, and Peter and Lenka are going to look after them," she said. "I know it is hard to understand, but I need you to be a big girl. Tomorrow, I need you to gather all your things that you want to take with you. The rest we will give away. Okay?"

I nodded in agreement, my mind swirling with information.

"Okay. Let's get you to bed," she said, as she walked me to the bedroom.

I lay in bed that night with my head spinning. Who were these bad people? If they are so bad to make us leave, what will happen to Grandma and Grandpa? What about the rest of our family? What about Radek? Has anyone told his family? What if they want to go, too? *A trip. A long trip.* Here, I thought we were going to Split. That is not that far. How long are we going for? Should I take all my toys? And we can't come back to this house. Where are we going to stay when we do come back? My mind was wandering in thought until I fell asleep.

6

The next day, Uncle Peter was there when I arrived at breakfast. He had obviously been deep in conversation with my parents because when I walked in, they got oddly loud in greeting me. I was getting used to the way everyone discussed things without me hearing. I didn't like it, but I was getting used to it.

Uncle Peter and my dad started moving furniture into a truck parked on the side of the road. My mother explained that Peter was going to keep some of our things with him until we could send for them.

"When you are done with your breakfast, I really need you to go through your things today and put whatever you don't want to keep in this box. Okay?" she asked as she placed the empty cardboard box on the table I sat at.

I nodded as I filled my mouth with the freshly baked rolls and soft, creamy cheese my parents had gotten that morning. The hot chocolate I sipped brought me comfort, as I prepared myself for the day.

The house was loud, with everyone coming and going. I retreated into the bedroom I shared with my parents. My twin-sized wooden bed and mattress were already gone, leaving only a dusty trace of where it once stood. My white wooden cabinet was still in its place. I opened the two small doors on its face and began to take out all my belongings. Stuffed toys, puzzles, games, books and crayons. I laid them all out on the floor. I stared at them for a good long time, feeling numb and lost. The questions didn't fill my head today. I was quiet and just going through the motions when I went to go get the cardboard box my mother had asked me to fill. I started with the obvious and placed my brick-red rabbit and my crying doll I had named Adelle into a pile of keepers. Without feeling, I began placing the toys I wanted to keep in one pile while putting the toys I haven't touched in a long time into the box. When I finished, I went and got my mother.

"This is all the stuff you don't want?" she asked in surprise. I barely realized that there were more toys I was giving away than keeping. I quietly nodded.

"Okay." she said shrugging her broad shoulders.

"Can I go play outside?" I asked.

"Yes, but please stay close," she insisted.

As I was putting on my shoes, I noticed she had taken out a couple of toys from my box and put them on her bed. I'm not sure why she did it, but I didn't care at this moment. I went down stairs and knocked on Radek's door. He answered and disappeared with me to our usual spot.

"You are very quiet today," he said.

I nodded.

"Is everything okay?" he asked.

"We are moving," I answered quietly.

"I know. My mother told me," he sadly replied.

"You knew?!" I shrieked. How could he have known and not told me!

"She told me this morning. I'm sorry. She said you were moving far away and we wouldn't get to hang out anymore," he said. "Don't be sad. We can still write each other. Mom said she is going to stay in touch with your parents, so we can send each other stuff."

"Okay," I said, feeling a little better about the situation. I wasn't going to lose my only friend.

We watched Uncle Peter and my parents bringing things down from the flat and loading them into the medium-sized blue truck until it seemed that the truck would tip over from the weight. The last thing I saw them load was the cardboard box of toys I had filled.

The last remaining days seemed to be a blur. The flat got emptier and emptier. My father's pile of money grew slowly but steadily, and I spent as much time as I could with Radek, although our time together was not like it used to be. It was quieter as if we were suddenly strangers in an awkward meeting. But his company made me feel more at ease. Both grandparents, Uncle Peter and Lenka stopped by at their own intervals to say their good-byes. They were full of sorrow and hesitation. I became immune to the feelings all the good-byes brought.

On the day we left the flat for the final time, I grabbed only one thing: my rabbit. On our way to the car, we stopped by Radek's flat. Our parents spoke and said their good-byes, as Radek gave me a small little picture of himself, and I promised to send him one of me so that we wouldn't forget each other. It was a short visit. As we walked to the car, I took one final glimpse of where our hangout used to be. Memories started flooding my mind. I was sad and held my rabbit closer to me as if he was my only happiness. My mother opened the rear side door of the car for me. I somehow expected our car to be stuffed, but there were only two suitcases by the side of the trunk and the backseat had my pillow and comforter. There must be more in the trunk already I thought but saw nothing more. I slid the pillow and comforter to one side and took my place on the tan leather seat, adjusting a few times to find a comfortable spot. My father loaded the car trunk, and my mother took her place in the passenger's seat. They looked at each other in silent confirmation and then both looked at me and smiled.

We were off.

7

The drive was long. I found myself fading in and out of sleep as we went. Each time I came to, the scenery was slightly different. City, then countryside, forest than a small town. We were headed for the Hungarian Border so we could cross into Yugoslavia.

I was tired and just like my thoughts, the Hungarian border came and went. Hungary's landscape was much like our own and kept me the same rhythm of fading in and out.

We arrived at a meeting point that my father had pre-arranged with the other family we were meeting. The Rihas.

They had two children my age. A daughter, Klara, with stunningly beautiful straight blonde hair, was a few months my senior. And a son, Zdenek, named after his father with dimples, which made his smile brighten the darkest of days, was a few months my junior. They were a nice family. Zdenek Senior was a husky man with dark thick hair and his wife Elena was of the same blonde, slender beauty that her daughter would inherit in years to come.

Their medium-sized Jeep Willis was packed to the limit. It was obvious they were headed somewhere and it drew attention. That was the first thing my father said. They spent the day reorganizing the car and making it look less obvious. Being of no help to them at all, Zdenek Jr., Klara, and I went to play. It was a hot day. We spent most of our time playing with tennis rackets as if we were trained tennis players, and the other half we spent soaked in water. I had made new friends and spent the day in comfortable ease.

We were to leave the following morning for the next stretch, Yugoslavia.

8

A voice woke me. A man's voice. He was asking for our papers. I was lying in an awkward position in the backseat with my head propped up by a pillow against the window, clinging to my rabbit. His deep voice stirred me to consciousness, but something told me not to open my eyes.

"Where are you going?" he demanded.

"Vacation to Split," said my mother quietly. "Could you please keep it down. My daughter is sleeping in the back," she added with a hint of courage in her tone.

I could feel his gaze on me. I lay there as still as I could, trying not to give my true state away. I felt something hard poking me through the cushion I sat on but pretended not to notice.

"What of the car?" he pressed on, quieter this time. I didn't understand the question, the pain from the cushion was getting worse, but I still refused to budge and clenched my eyes closed even more.

"They were having car trouble, so we are helping them tow. They are going to the same place," my mother answered.

I was dying to see this man's face and see my surroundings, but I dared not look. The talking had stopped and it was only minutes before I felt the car move forward again and pick up speed, only then did I have the courage to crack open an eye to see where we were. The Yugoslavian boarder. I noticed that another car was attached to ours in the back. Upon closer inspection, I realized it was the Rihas sitting inside it. The red wooden beam closed behind our cars as they cleared us to pass, men in green uniforms slowly walking about the area. I couldn't tell which one of them had been the one staring at me through the back window, but I was glad it was over. My mother put away our light grey passports and seemed to sigh with relief.

Split was beautifully tropical. We had stayed there two years ago and several times before that. Sunny and warm with bone-white sand that glistened in the sun. We had been guests of a family that lived on the beach. They had a simple little house with a trail that led directly onto the beach. Just at the edge of their property, they had a huge tent set up. I had never seen a tent like that. The front of the tent had a hallway that held all the kitchen equipment and the back had beds. The one really obvious thing about our living quarters that year was the odd number of cats in the area. They were everywhere. Flee infested stray cats that wandered the property and snuck their way into our beds when we left the door open. There was a constant smell in the air. It was sweet yet pungent, like fruit going bad. Hot figs. There were massive fig trees the size of elephants along the beach. They had held onto fruit the size of tennis balls, but no one seemed to be eating them fast enough. The limbs were bent under the weight of the oversized fruit. It made the tree look like a sagging pepper tree. I remember my mother picked a fresh one for me. I had to hold it with both hands. It was so big, but when I bit into it, it was like warm honey; sweet, juicy, and full of flavor. I definitely got my fill of fig from these abundant trees that year.

We were passing that area today. The orange sun was starting to set and it seemed my father was looking for a specific address. Within minutes, we had arrived. The two-story bungalows were made of stone, almost white with brown trim. They were small and stacked close to each other along the pier. There were rows of them with water channeling between each pier. Delicate bright red and purple flowers decorated the walls and roofs of each bungalow. They looked like something out of a storybook. We got out of the car and took only our immediate suitcases. I followed my father to the bungalow that we were to stay in, with my rabbit at my side. He knocked on the door to the bungalow that read "Manager," A frail old man opened the door with a big smile on his face. "About time you guys got here!" he exclaimed, "let me show you to the bungalow you guys will be in," He closed the door and escorted us to a bungalow, two doors down. He unlocked the door for us and we entered. It was small but cute. The room had a small kitchen with a table and chairs and a staircase in the far left corner. "Let me know if you need anything" he said "I took the liberty to grab you some basic foods for tonight and there is a little store at the end of the beach for anything you might need in the morning." With that he left us to escort the Rihas to the one they would be in, but my father followed him out. I could hear them talking outside the door of the bungalow, but couldn't make out what they were saying. Before I could investigate further, my mother grabbed my attention. "Let's go see what is upstairs," she said, taking me gently by the shoulder and moving me to the back of the small bungalow.

We walked upstairs to find a large room with a couple of beds and some dressers. There was a small window that overlooked the water, which was blackening in the setting evening sun. There was nothing else to see up here. My mother had brought up the smaller of the luggage with us and was rummaging through it on one of the beds. "Let's find the bathroom and get you washed up," she said. There was no bathroom upstairs, so we headed back down the solid wooden stairs. The room downstairs was about the same size. No living area, just a wooden dining set for four people and a small kitchen. There was a door in the kitchen I had not noticed before. It was an old looking door. I opened it slowly with curiosity. "I found the bathroom!" I hollered at my mother. It was a tiny bathroom. A sink, toilet and small corner shower with a curtain hanging in front of it. She was behind me within moments holding my pajamas and a handful of toiletries. "Well, this is not bad," she said, although the look on her face seemed to indicate otherwise. She began walking me through the rituals of preparing for bed. I had not eaten, but I was too tired to even complain.

9

In the morning, I got up. A wide ray of sun was staring at me from the small drapeless window and provoked me to open my eyes and rise. I was the only one upstairs. I put on my slippers that my mother had left for me and headed down stairs. I found my mother in the kitchen. She was putting away breakfast and preparing a cup of something. Smelled like hot chocolate. "Good morning, sunshine, I thought I heard you up there," she said without turning around. As I approached the little bathroom, she turned and smiled. "Breakfast is on the table for you." I could barely comprehend her words and I dragged my tired legs into the bathroom. I began my morning ritual that mother had instilled in me. Wash my face, brush my hair, brush my teeth, and so on. After I completed my ritual, I came out to find a steaming cup of hot chocolate on the table next to a couple slices of rye bread dressed with ham and Swiss cheese. I sat down.

"Where is dad?" I asked.

"He went to the beach with Zdenek a few hours ago," she said. "When you are all done, we will head over there to meet up with them,"

The beach! How exciting! I hadn't been since the last time we were in Split. This would be a lot of fun! My mind was suddenly wide awake, and I ate my breakfast with vigor. Everything tasted so good! Within moments, my breakfast was gone and I hurried upstairs to change into the day's clothes. "Put on your swimsuit, it is in the brown bag and your shorts!" my mother hollered as she cleared the table. Upstairs, I rummaged through the bag she described. I grabbed my swimsuit, a pair of shorts, and a shirt. I was ready, but she was not. She made me wait what seemed like hours while she collected her things and some foods. She was killing me! Let's go! I thought… we are losing time. Finally, she said the words I had been waiting for. "Okay, are you ready?"

"Yes!" I exclaimed. Ready? I had been ready!

We started walking from our bungalow back to the shoreline and turned right onto a cement walkway. We walked past several bungalow piers and past a group of fishing boats that sat in the harbor. After a while, I spotted it! White sand that sparkled in the morning sun. It was a fairly short stretch, not like the beach we had been to a couple years ago, and there were very few people there. As we approached, my mother picked out a spot and laid down a blanket for us to sit on. I removed my shorts and shoes and plopped down on the brown blanket. The heat of the sand had already penetrated the thin blanket and was now actively warming my legs. I looked around, inspecting the area I was to spend time in. There were no children my age on the beach today. It was mostly older couples strolling along. The water was as still as glass with small splashing waves along the shore. I could see a couple silhouettes in the distance playing in the water. They were too far away to recognize faces, but they were obviously there. They held on to two beautifully colored sails. Large sails. One was red and orange stripped and the other was all yellow. They seemed to reach for the sky as if they hoped to touch it and the bottoms lay anchored against the water. They only stayed in the air for moments at a time before falling flat against the water, taking the silhouettes with them. I watched with curiosity as the silhouettes struggled to get the sails upright and stand on the glassy water. After a few minutes of this repetitive action, I realized they weren't standing on the water at all, they were standing on some kind of a long board.

"Do you see him?" my mother asked. I looked at her in confusion. "I think he is on the red and orange wind surfer. They wanted to give it a try." She said pointing at the objects I had been obsessed with for the last few minutes. "They don't seem to be very good at it. It was probably a bad day to try wind sailing since there is no wind," she said laughing.

I gazed in amazement. That was my father out there. He was on the red and orange one, which means Zdenek must be on the yellow one. I smiled as I realized how funny they looked trying to learn to use those sails, but I felt a slight hint of pride, knowing that he was trying to conquer something new. I watched him for most of the morning, enthralled and silently cheering him on. My mother was stretched out on the blanket with her face covered by a shirt, basking in the morning heat. A few moments later, I heard a familiar voice. "Hi, guys!" It was Elena and with her were Zdenek Jr. and Klara. They were dressed in swimsuits and Elena's thin body bore a small, white linen dress over her black bikini. They approached us and settled in next to our blanket. My mother sat up and started talking to Elena, while I started sharing my story of watching our fathers try to wind surf.

"Can we go wind surf?" Zdenek Jr. exclaimed. What a great idea! Why had I not thought of that?

"No. You guys are too young for that," said Elena.

I was a bit disappointed, but it passed almost as quickly as it came. We spent the day on that beach. Nibbling on snacks and exploring the shore and the water nearest the blankets we had nestled into the bright warm sand. My mother and Elena had parked themselves on the blankets and sunbathed, only glancing at us every so often to make sure we were not getting into trouble. We had a great time on that shore, no cares or worries in the world. We were in happy bliss. I remember looking at my father ever so often, still finding them struggling with their sails. We kept cheering for them. It was the game of the day. They only stayed up for a few seconds and then a couple minutes at a time. It was amusing to watch. Unfortunately, the day ended as quickly as it came. Elena took Zdenek Jr. and Klara back to the bungalows to wash up for dinner, but my mother let us stay. I ended that day the same way it had started. Sitting on that warm blanket watching my father tackle the stubborn sail. The sun started to set, and an orange glow surrounded them in dark silhouette. A breeze started to form and for the first time, the sails grabbed hold of it like it was the difference between life and death and took the silhouettes for a ride. For the first time all day, I watched my father surf the black, glassy ocean clinging to his sail for several minutes before being consumed by the dark waters. I jumped and cheered for him! He had done it! I don't know if he had heard me from that far away, but I believed he heard me in spirit. The sun set fast and my mother beckoned me to go. I watched him until the very last second until the groupings of boats in the harbor hid him from view. I was proud of his achievements and happily walked back to the bungalow. That night at dinner, I listened to the tales my father shared of how he struggled with the sails and why and how it was so much harder then it seems but that he wasn't willing to give up. That was a trait I found in my father all the time. He never gave up until he accomplished what he set out to do. I listened until I could listen no more, and my happy mind went blank and my tired eyes closed for the day.

10

I awoke the next morning in my temporary bed. I lay there thinking about the dreams I had of windsurfing with my father into unknown lands. As my mind became more awake, my dreams seemed to fade into a lost memory. I got up. My parents were downstairs at the table drinking coffee and talking. There was a map laid out, and they seemed to be making plans.

"Good morning," said my father as I entered the downstairs.

"Morning," I replied with half a yawn.

"Do you want hot chocolate or tea for breakfast?" my mother asked.

"Hot chocolate," I replied as I made my way to the bathroom for my morning ritual. I was slightly red in the mirror this morning from being out in the sun all day, but nothing hurt, so I dismissed it.

Other than the fact that we ate together, breakfast was pretty uneventful. I was told to get dressed and go with my father today. I was excited at the idea of spending the day with him and hurried to get ready. When I came downstairs, he was already standing outside the door. I walked outside to join him and he handed me a short metal rod with a nylon string hanging from it. "Ready?" he asked.

"What is this?" I asked.

"It's a fishing rod. We are going to catch some fish for lunch," he said with an excited smile.

Fishing?! I had never tried that before, nor had I ever seen my father fish. I was bursting with excitement. I happily skipped alongside my father as he walked the pier to a little store made of grey stone. We went inside, and my father purchased a little tin can of bait. We walked the cement pier for quite some time until my father found a spot that he liked and we settled there. He was going to show me how to bait my hook. As he opened the little tin can, which was no bigger than the palm of his hand, my eyes widened at the site of the fleshy, wiggly mush that he exposed. They were worms! Live worms! He pulled three out and put them in the palm of my little hand. They squirmed in the sun, almost falling past my tiny fingers. I couldn't possibly put them on my hook like my father instructed. Smiling, my father took one of the worms I held and carefully showed me how to put the dark red worm on the silver little hook he had placed on the nylon line earlier. He did so with quiet poise and determination. Once baited, he took the other two worms out of my hand, placing one back in the little tin can, rejoining the rest of the dark red wiggling mass, and the other on the end of the little silver hook of the black fishing pole he had reserved for himself. He then took hold of my hands, wrapped them around the pole, his thin, long hands consuming my own, and showed me how to launch my fishing line before launching his own. "Now what?" I asked.

"Now we wait," he said smiling.

We sat on the pier waiting for a fish. My father instructed me on what to do if I caught a one and then what we would do with it after we actually caught a fish. He said the goal was to catch at least three fish, one for each of us. After about a half hour, we had to rebait the hooks and repeat the whole process. We were there for a long time with no success. Finally, my father moved us to a different area of the same pier. We repeated the ritual of getting the baited hooks into the water and then sat and waited in quiet comfort. Unlike my mother, my father was a quiet man only speaking when he had something to say. I found a certain comfort in this quality. It made me comfortable to be in silence and confidant to be in my own skin. We sat there silently watching the seagulls fight the waves for their next meal, watching the puffy clouds change form in the pale blue sky, the sun dance on the calm ocean sea and admiring the beauty of the day. I soaked in this quiet time with my father. Then, all of a sudden, a pull. My fishing rod tensed and the reel spun and then stopped. "Hurry!" my father exclaimed in a whisper, "grab the rod and slowly reel him in." I nervously grabbed the rod and started reeling. Within seconds, my father's hands, strong and firm, were around mine on the reel, he was helping me through the motions. Within seconds, a fish flew out of the dark ocean and dangled in the air attached to the nylon string my rod was holding. It squirmed and tossed in the air as my father grabbed the line and drew it in. As soon as he did, his fishing rod tensed and his reel spun. He left go of my fish and grabbed his fishing rod. I starred at the helpless fish tossing on the cement, still attached to the line and rod I held. It was a flat, silver-looking fish about the size of my father's large hands. Within moments, my father had taken his fish and mine off the hooks and, with a huge smile on his face, he rehooked them side by side on a thick piece of rope about six feet long with several hooks embedded in the two feet at its end. Rehooked, he placed the rope into the water. Seeing the confusion on my face, he explained, "It will keep them fresh until we are ready to leave. Only two more to go," He said excitedly.

I rebaited my line on my own this time, working the wiggling worm around my hook for several minutes until my father approved my efforts and then we relaunched our lines. We again sat in simple quietness, but, this time, there was a sense of accomplishment in my heart and my father turned to me and rubbed my head in pride. I could tell he was happy and that made me happy, too. After a while, we caught another fish and added it to the rope sitting in the water. When we had our four, my father looked at me and asked, "Do you want to stay and try to catch a couple more?" He seemed to really be enjoying the process and if that was the excuse I needed to just spend a few more moments with him, then so be it. We stayed on the pier until the sun started getting that orangish afternoon glow and then gathered our things and headed back to the quiet bungalow. When we arrived, my mother was outside with a long knife and a large, wooden, cutting board. She placed it on the small wooden bench, which sat against the white retaining wall across from the bungalow. She smiled as we approached.

"I was beginning to worry. That was supposed to be for lunch. How did you do?" she asked with a big smile.

"We caught ten fish!" I exclaimed as my father raised the fish studded rope pride for her to view.

"We were having some trouble at first and then had to move to a different spot, so it took a little longer than I had expected," he explained.

"Wow! That is great!" she cried "Here is a wooden board and a sharp knife so you can prep the fish," she said to my father. "Let's get you cleaned up," she said to me.

As my father placed his fish on the bench and started arranging his designated tools, I followed my mother into the bungalow. I washed up and changed my clothes. By the time I rejoined my father outside, he had cleaned all the fish and was chatting happily with Zdenek. The two men walked into the bungalow to hand off the fish to my mother and I followed.

"You are quite the fisherman," Zdenek said to me "Your father was telling me how many fish you caught on your first trip. It's very impressive." I smiled, gleaming with pride.

"I invited Zdenek and his family to join us, so go ahead and cook them all. There are plenty to go around and we can't save them for tomorrow," my father said to my mother.

We all feasted on the grilled fish we had caught and boiled potatoes that evening. My father bragged on my fish catching, and I ate up the praise with vigor. I couldn't tell if I was blushing with pride or if my face was feeling the effects of the hot afternoon sun. Either way, it was a satisfaction I clung to.

11

The next morning, my mother woke me up. It was time to go. I felt a tinge of sadness, it had been a long time since I had had that kind of time with my father and I felt like it would be a while before I could have that back again. Reluctantly, I got up and went about my routine. Everything was already packed and on its way to the car by the time I was done with my bread and hot chocolate. My mother quickly washed the dishes I had been using, walked the bungalow one last time, collected the last of her things, and walked me to the car. Zdenek was parked next to us and stuffing his car with the last of their luggage. His family was already seated in the car. My mother spread out a large paper map of Yugoslavia and Austria in front of her and guided my father to an address she had jotted down. The Rihas were in tow behind us. A half an hour later, we arrived at a farm-looking two-story house. The land around the house was covered in various shades of green and a scattering of delicate white flowers. A middle-aged man in blue overalls was waiting on the grassy area in front of the house. My father pulled the car up to the house via the gravel road and got out of the car. Zdenek did the same. The three men spoke. I could see money was being exchanged and then the man pointed to the side of the house. As Zdenek and my father returned to the car, I looked to my mother.

"What is going on? Who is that?" I asked.

"It is a man that is going to sell us some gasoline for the car," my mother replied.

I didn't understand why we were getting gasoline from him when we had always gotten our gasoline at a gas station. And why were they paying with cash, they always paid using these funny-looking coupons. I had seen them do it many times before. Curiosity finally got the best of me and I mustered up the courage to ask. "Don't we usually get gas at a gas station?"

My mother fell silent for a moment and looked to my father who had gotten back in the car and preparing to drive it to the spot the man had indicated. My father looked at me through the rear view mirror. "We don't have any more gas vouchers Lucie, so this man is going to sell us some of his gas from his farm."

Gas vouchers? Those must be the coupons I've seen them use. I had pressed the matter far enough and wasn't willing to ask any more questions on the matter. My father pulled up to a huge rusty metal tank that sat next to a dark grey wooden barn. He parked the car and got out. The man that had greeted him on the porch was now standing by the side of the tank, filling a smaller plastic container that he handed to my father as he approached. "Fill her up and bring it back," he said. My father took the gas filled container and walked it to our car. I could hear him opening the gas cap and pouring the liquid in. He repeated the process several times until the tank was full. Then it was Zdenek's turn. As he went about the same routine, my father talked to the man and my mother got out of the car to join him. I cranked down my manual window and sat as close as I could to the door so that I could hear what was being said.

"That should be enough gas to get you over the border. You don't need gas vouchers in Austria. That is just a socialist thing. Austria is all capitalist, so you should have no problems," I heard the man say, "Just in case, though, here are a couple of our vouchers. We have the tank, so we don't use as many," he said as he handed my father two gas vouchers.

Their conversation was followed by a barrage of "thank you" from my father, my mother, and Zdenek. They exchanged a few more words and then we were back on the road. This time, the drive was much further.

12

I watched the green scenery go by as if in a trance and that old unsettling feeling started creeping up on me again. I knew there were things that my parents were not telling me, but I didn't have the courage to ask. As if instinct took over, I drew my rabbit closer to me for comfort.

After what seemed like hours, we arrived at the Yugoslavian/Austrian border. The air in the car stiffened as we approached. I felt the tension and held my breath. As we approached the red and white patrol gate, I could see a patrol man in green uniform bending over the side of a small black car filled with two attractive looking women, who apparently were trying to pass as well. They were talking and laughing, and in no hurry to let us through. As my father slowed the car down to stop behind them, I saw flashing headlights behind us. Zdenek. My father rolled his window down and looked behind the car at Zdenek, who was leaning as far as he could out of his rolled down window, yelling at the top of his lungs, "Go, Joe! For God's sakes. Go! Step on it!"

Without hesitation, my father pulled the car to the right, catching the tall green and yellow grass and passing the car with the two women. He drove around the red and white patrol gate as fast as he could get the car to go, gravel and dirt flying behind us. Zdenek being pulled close at our heels. The last thing we heard was the sound of a whistle being blown frantically by the white faced, frantic man in uniform. I looked back and behind Zdenek's car, I could see the patrolman flagging down someone in the distance. My father was going fast, as fast as I had ever seen him go. I clung to the small tan headrest in front of me. My mother was frantic but supporting my father's actions. "We just have to make it to the other side of the border!" she exclaimed!

As her words echoed in my mind, the piercing sound of police cars replaced it. I looked behind us and I could see police cars approaching fast, lights blazing and sirens screaming. At first, there was only one, then two, I looked in front of us and we were approaching a cement bridge that we had to cross at all costs. Our plans were involuntarily changed, and my father slammed on the brakes. They were rebuilding it, and the side we needed to cross was full of workers. There was a tall beer-bellied man at the front of the bridge holding a pole with a red and white stop sign and ran toward us trying to slow us down. We couldn't cross. My father reluctantly stopped the car. My mother burst out of the passenger's seat and ran to the man with the sign frantically yelling, "Please let us pass. We are trying to escape, please! We are seeking asylum! We are seeking asylum! Please!"

Five police cars were flashing their lights in the distance, their sirens drowning out the sound of my mother's words and getting louder as they were fast approaching.

"Please!" Her pleas were unanswered as the poor man holding the sign stood there, wide-eyed at my mother's frantic cries, shrugging his shoulders and pointing at the bridge and the passing cars and shaking his head, helpless. Within seconds, seven police cars surrounded us, their sirens were now deafening in my ears. They rushed out of their cars and drew their shotguns at the windows that protected my father and Zdenek. Two police officers ran toward my mother yelling at her to get her hands up and get down on the ground. She kneeled and raised her arms, her back toward us as the man with the stop sign retreated to the protection of his post at the bridge. The policeman yelled at my father and Zdenek. I wanted to help my mother but I was too scared. I wanted to yell and scream, but I resorted to silently clinging to my rabbit, trying to hold it together as I watched the policeman handcuff my mother. As he walked her past our car, I could see her now flushed face, twisted with anguish and streams of tears rolling down her terrified but defeated face. She was pleading with the police officer in vein as he placed her in the back of his car. The police then put their guns away and instructed my father to follow them to the station. Having no choice and concerned about my mother, my father agreed. I sat silent in the backseat. I wanted to comfort him or say something that would make the moment easier to deal with, but I couldn't find the words. Then the anguish got the best of me, and all of a sudden it was me that needed comforting. My eyes welled up with silent tears.

My fathered followed the two police cars to the station while the rest of the cars followed us. The first car, which held my mother, continued on and disappeared around the corner. The car my father was following pulled up along the curb in front of the border patrol station just before the corner the first car had rounded. My father pulled up behind it, and the other cars followed in line. The policeman got out of the car in front of us and approached my father's window, which he instinctively rolled down.

"Open the trunk and get out of the vehicle," said the patrolman.

My father got out of the car to open the trunk. I could not see what they were doing, but it was obvious he was searching the vehicle. The car moved around as he rustled through the baggage, finally closing the trunk.

"Papers?" he demanded.

My father returned to the interior and rummaged in the car for the government-issued documents we had received and our passports. After handing the policeman the papers, he instructed my father, who then walked around the side of the car and opened my door motioning me to get out.

I was scared and I found myself forgetting to breathe as my father took me by the hand. I looked to my father for guidance, but he had fear and worry written all over his face. He looked to Zdenek, who was surrounded by police. They were being forced to exit the car, too, and had begun a search of their vehicle.

"Come with me," he said to my father. "You too," indicating the Rihas family. He walked us inside the building and sat us down in an open cement cell. I sat next to my father, on a metal bench that the cell had several of, quietly clinging to my rabbit. What was going to happen? The officer closed the iron cell door and left. Where was my mother?

We sat in the cold cell quietly waiting. After a few minutes, another policeman in green uniform and matching hat approached the cell looking through the pages of paperwork that my father and Zdenek had handed over and stared at us, with his stern and icy eyes, for a moment before speaking.

"What was your purpose in trying to enter Austria?" he demanded.

"We are on vacation," My father replied.

"Your papers are only for entry into Yugoslavia," He commanded and waited for a response. When my father didn't give one, he proceeded, "Are you aware that it is illegal for you to go beyond your sanctioned area?" he asked almost looking forward to the power that gave him.

"What do you mean?" my father asked.

"Your government has a law in place. You are only allowed to enter countries that you have written government permission to enter," he said nonchalantly. "Do you have this written permission to enter Austria?"

"No. I'm sorry, we were not aware," My father answered, and then changed the subject. "May I ask where my wife is?"

"Your wife is being held in custody until this matter is resolved," he stated matter of factly. "We are under strict orders to arrest anyone trying to leave Czechoslovakia without the proper documentation and turn them over to Czechoslovakian police for processing."

My father sat still and quiet. Now what? They had arrested my mother and were going to turn us in, which meant we would all be arrested for desertion.

"We were not aware, sir. We were just going on a family vacation," my father pleaded.

But he was aware, I thought. *I heard you talk about it.* He was lying. I was always told not to ever lie, but he was. Maybe there is a time when it is okay to lie, I considered that statement. Like now.

"And you were on vacation with them?" he asked Zdenek, who had been silently watching the situation.

"Yes, we were on vacation," Zdenek responded.

The officer stared at us, with a sinister smile on his face, for a few moments longer, shuffled through our documents again, and, without saying a word, he left. We sat there waiting for what seemed like hours. My mother was nowhere to be found. I was scared, and the cold from the metal bench had penetrated my clothing and began to freeze my buttocks and thighs, but didn't want to add to my father's problems as I could tell he was scared, too. What if they find the stitching in the seats? I knew my father was thinking the same. What would happen to us? Minutes turned into hours. We sat there alone waiting.

Various men in green uniform kept coming to look in on us, giggling, whispering. and pointing, just to taunt us for several hours. Finally, one of the policemen, with a mature yet kinder face, seemed to take pity on us. He disappeared for only a moment before returning with our documents in his hand. He opened the iron cell door and asked us all to follow him. He walked us into a large office that housed a file-filled desk, filing cabinets, and several chairs facing it. My mother sat on one of these cushioned chairs. She was no longer her put-together self. Her face was flushed and swollen, and tears refused to leave her now puffy eyes. She held an overused cloth handkerchief that she was wiping her eyes with when she saw us enter. She jumped up and hugged my father and then me with strength and purpose. The policeman closed the door behind us and looked at all of us for a second, finally resting his pale blue eyes on my father. "Do you have money?" he asked.

My mother searched the officer's round face. "No. We only have a very small amount," she pleaded.

"We have money," Zdenek interrupted. My mother's gaze darted to him. I couldn't read what she was thinking, but fear had become even more prominent on her face.

"Look," he said, his face softening, "they've done the background research and realize you are of no threat. If you have money, I will sell you a three-day pass into Austria. If you can reach the refugee camp within that time and register, you will be fine. If not, you will be escorted back to Czechoslovakia and dealt with by the police there," he stated, searching our faces for a response.

Finally, my mother seemed to come out of a daze and responded, "Yes!" then catching herself, "Yes, we will take the pass."

"Very well, follow me," he said to my mother, "the rest of you wait here."

After he and my mother left, the heaviness of the air lifted and everyone found a place to sit while we waited for their return. The conversations began.

"Will that be enough time, you think?" Zdenek asked.

"It should be if we don't make any extra stops," my father answered.

"I wonder how much they are going to ask for," Zdenek said, looking for some kind of an answer from my father, but he did not give one.

After a while, the officer returned with my mother. She was holding everyone's passports and started distributing them to the parents. She seemed to still be shaken up, but much more put together than she had been earlier.

"Let's go," the policeman politely motioned to the door. We all got up and followed his stout figure out the door and into the cream-colored hall and then outside where our cars stood. "Good luck," he said with a nod and partial smile, turned, and left us standing on the curb.

My father took me by the hand and we walked toward our car, in front of which lay all our belongings from the detailed search they had done of the cars in our absence. My mother started reorganizing the luggage and my father put the pieces back in the car, while the Rihas did the same. They had not found the items in the seats and I took my place upon them as if my presence would protect them. My mother started fixing her teary face in the passenger's seat to regain her composure while my father helped the Rihas get their vehicle in its earlier state.

We pulled out of the station on the other side of the red and white patrol bar and proceeded to retrace our drive to the Austrian border, making it across the bridge that had been our defeat, with calmness and ease. We had made it. We were in Austria. My father drove for a good while, gaining distance between us and the border, and bringing us as close to our destination as possible before stopping for a break.

13

The orange sun was setting behind the green hills, which were now turning black as it started to get dark. We found a little inn nearby and spent the night. I remember everyone sleeping in the next morning as if the events of the prior day had exhausted everyone's efforts to push forward. I was up first. I lay in bed waiting to hear a stir from my parents. My mind wandered to yesterday. The fear and tension I had hid inside suddenly came to me full strength and I laid there crying silently to myself. I couldn't help it, couldn't stop it, but I stayed quiet. Not wanting to disturb my sleeping parents. I tried to think of other things. Grandpa, fruit-filled dumplings, swans. I stopped crying but the sadness wouldn't leave me. I stared at the ceiling, wiping my tears with my blanket for only a few moments before I got up. Quietly as a mouse, I began looking for clean clothes, but quiet or not, my mother was awake. "Let me help you," she whispered. "We should get up anyways," and with that she shook my father awake and began the process of getting going again. We had breakfast on the wooden patio of the inn that overlooked a small lake nestled between the rolling hills. Breakfast tasted extra good today. The small white eggs, that were soft boiled, housed the darkest and sweetest yolk I had ever encountered. They served freshly baked bread rolls whose fragrant steam rolled past my nose and homemade strawberry jam that had more strawberry chunks than jam. But nothing compared to the boiled over chocolate milk that nurtured my taste buds with ever sip. Breakfast filled our bellies and lifted our spirits. Within an hour, we were back on the road, the Rihas in tow, as if the Inn were just a passing thought now.

The scenery was densely green with pastures, forests, meadows, and dark-blue lakes that entertained me on the drive. We passed through small stucco-filled villages here and there and stopped once for lunch before the skies grew dark. By mid afternoon, the clouds had rolled in and the rain had started to fall, causing it to get prematurely dark. My mother was intently following the instructions on her map of the area and cross-checking her position with the blue and white street signs, whenever she could find some. Night came quickly but according to my mother, we weren't far from our destination, and my father wanted to press on and get there as soon as possible before the weather got any worse. As if reading his thoughts, the skies lit up with shards of lightening and a full down pour of rain took its vengeance upon us. Thunder crashed over us, and my father was forced to slow down so that he could see. His headlights could only penetrate the first few feet of rain, and he had to make sure we were on the road, especially with the Rihas still in tow. It was suddenly cold, and I curled up in the thick down comforter my mother had put in the backseat for me earlier. Its heaviness and comfort must have caused me to doze off because my mother's startled yelp woke me to full consciousness. I looked around to see what was going on. We were surrounded by dark sinister silhouettes that slowly approached the car. They wore tree branches and were smeared with dirt. Wet from the rain, holding rifles and approaching the vehicle as if we were prey, I realized they were men in camouflage. My father suddenly rolled the window down.

"Who are you? What are you doing here?" the soldier demanded in German.

"We are lost" my mother said in German, leaning over my father to see the man, "We are trying to find Traiskirchen."

My parents, like most of the citizens of Czechoslovakia, were required to learn several languages in school and spoke almost fluent German and Russian. She had started teaching me basics at a very early age.

"Traiskirchen?!" the man exclaimed almost laughing, "You are in the middle of a drill on a military base. We almost shot you!" He shook his head in disbelief.

"Can you help us get back on the right road?" my father asked.

"You scared us," my mother laughed nervously. "The rain is coming down so hard we couldn't see and there are almost no signs anywhere."

The broad-chested man smiled under all the wet mud on his face, causing his features to be completely hidden from view. He turned toward the headlights in the distance and hollered something, and then spoke into his radio. The twigs on his head hitting the top of our car as he did so. "Follow that car up there," he said to my father as he pointed to the yellow set of headlights. "They will guide you off the base. Traiskirchen is on the other side of those hills about 20 minutes. About 10 minutes from where they will leave you."

"Thank you. Thank you so much," my mother cried.

The man nodded and stepped away so that my father could proceed as he proceeded to talk into his radio some more. Slowly making his way to the headlights in the distance, my parents were nervously laughing about the incident.

"He scared me!" my mother laughed, "all those branches they were wearing and the camouflage. Then when I noticed the guns, I thought we were in serious trouble."

My father acknowledged her statements and smiled but was focused on cautiously driving the car. The headlights turned into a small military truck and it turned around in front of us so we could follow it through a series of hidden turns to get us out of the area. At the top of the gentle hill, they pulled off the side of the road next to a check in booth, dark with no workers, and saluted us from inside the drenched truck. That was our sign to keep going apparently because my father politely saluted back and started the gentle downhill drive. Soon the streets were lit again and the rain had settled into gentle tapping against the windows of the car. In front of us, about 100 yards was a large yellow building with lights on and a heavy iron gate. The large metal sign outside read Traiskirchen. This was the refugee camp my parents were trying to get to. We had made it. I felt relieved and collapsed into my seat until we had fully arrived.

The next thing I knew, we were inside the cream-painted building filling out papers and being stocked with blankets, pillows, metal plates, and utensils along with a toothbrush and some smaller odds and ends before being escorted to one of the many rooms that lined the halls. The room we ended up in was full of wooden beds and bunks and in them other people, families like ours, settling in to sleep. The public bathrooms had no showers, only sinks and toilets laid upon an old tiled floor, but at that point, we were too tired to care. We quietly washed up and put an end to the long day.

14

Morning was chaos with so many people using the facilities. I stayed close to my parents during breakfast, which was heavily portioned and quite decent, before we were called to the main office for pictures and processing. It took quite a while to get through everything, but in the end, we ended up in an interview room following lunch. The man asked my parents many questions, where we wanted to go, where we were from, what our background was. It was all information to make sure we were who we said we were and to determine sponsorship and asylum placement. I didn't really know what that meant. I thought this was the destination we were trying to reach. To my dismay, it sounded as though our journey had not ended.

At dinner, we reunited with the Rihas and exchanged stories. They went through a similar evaluation process, and, by the end of the day, we had all been registered and accepted into the facility. By tomorrow, we would have asylum. I still didn't understand what that word meant, but it was becoming a regular part of my family's vocabulary.

Two days later, we were told we had received a sponsor and were given asylum to a place called Ramsau. We were to leave that afternoon, but the Rihas were not going with us. Their location had not been chosen yet. Directly following lunch, we turned in our blankets, pillows, and everything else we were issued on our arrival. We were given asylum cards that had our pictures, names, and personal information, and they escorted us to a bus waiting outside the building. When we got to the bus, a short man in slacks and a yellow shirt, stood in front and called out our last name.

"I understand you have a car here?" he asked without feeling or looking up from his paperwork.

"Yes," my father replied.

"Please collect your car and follow this bus to your location. Pull up behind the bus as soon as you are ready," he said and then proceeded to call out another name.

My parents took me gently by the hand and we walked to the parking lot behind the bus to retrieve our car. He must have visited the car before because Zdenek's car was no longer attached to the back of ours. We took our places in the car and within moments, my father pulled up behind the bus. The man that had called out our name walked up to the car and copied down the license plate. His face was thick with beady eyes that were only visible above the rims of his gold wire reading glasses. He proceeded to do the same with two other vehicles that suddenly appeared behind us. Finally, he disappeared into the pale green bus and returned without the stack of papers he had had in his thick hands. He waved to us and retreated into the building. The bus took off, and each car behind the bus proceeded with caution. We were on our way to another location. I went along, observing and absorbing everything and everyone around me, but I felt numb inside. I went through the motions and did as I was told.

The city we were in turned into lush countryside again and then dense, and somewhat dark, forest, into which the bus we were following slowly turned left, balancing from tire to tire as it left the smoothness of the road and secured its position on the gravel path through the tree. I questioned whether there was even a road there. We drove for quite some time before the light of the sun returned to our path, and the bus made another left turn into a large clearing. I stared out the window. There was a pretty creek with a small bridge, a large meadow with a pasture of multicolored cows and a beautiful dark green, thick forest on the left. On the right, there was a huge, tall-grassed hill with a large wooden sign depicting a fat cook's head and chef's hat, and to the right of his head were the words "Penzion Adamtal." As the bus passed the sign, it exposed a building. Mostly white with dark brown shutters, trim and fencing with bright red flowers dangling from the brown wooden window boxes under each window. It was a big place and very pleasing to the eyes. The bus was steadily slowing down until it came to a full stop directly in front of the main doors. My father pulled up behind it.

"I guess this is it," he said to my mother.

They stared at it for a moment. Out of the building came a husky older man in slacks and a light windbreaker waddling quickly to the bus. He waved to the bus and beckoned everyone to enter. As he did so, he continued approaching our car. He came upon my father's side of the car, out of breath and struggling to hold his large belly up. My father rolled the window down.

"Please park your car on the other side of the bus. There is a parking lot there. Park and then come inside," he said, as he pointed past the bus. My father acknowledged and started the car again. As he made his way around the bus, I could see the husky man approach each of the other cars and motion for them to park.

There were a lot of pine trees in the area. My father parked the car in the parking lot, which was positioned in front of an old, low-ceiling storage barn. It didn't seem to fit the rest of the building. It was made entirely of wood that had blackened from years of exposure to the elements. Some sections were missing, and you could see inside should you get close enough. It did not match the new and elegant feel of the main building. Everything around it, though, was really green and beautiful. We got out of the car and were met with a slight chill in the air. Not a warm breeze like we had in Split. We gathered our luggage and proceeded to the front door.

Just before we stepped inside, we were greeted by another sign, this one was almost as tall as me and all black board. It depicted a chef pointing at writing to the right of his finger, where something was written in white chalk on the black background. The building was clean and inviting. Everything was built with a light-colored wood with dark knots scattered upon it. The floor, banister, counters, tables, everything. There was a large room to the right of the check-in desk that had lots of tables and red leather chairs and served as the restaurant on site. I suddenly felt a tinge of hunger, and my belly rumbled. We waited in line, as each person was checked in by the older blonde woman at the counter and given a room. Ours was upstairs, second room from the staircase banister.

It was a large room, much bigger than we thought we were going to get. It had a very large bed against the left wall that featured the same light colored wood as the rest of the inn. There was a square table with a white square tablecloth draping it and a couple matching chairs, upon which I sat my red, tropically dressed rabbit, and a private bathroom. We entered the room and settled in. It took us several hours to unpack everything and get comfortable. Then there was a knock on the door. My mother opened it, and the same older blonde woman handed her a white standard-sized envelope. She thanked her, closed the wooden door and proceeded to inspect the contents of the envelope. It seemed to just be a bunch of paperwork, but I still watched as she shuffled through it. My father returned to the room shortly after bringing in the last of the items from the car, including my pillow and blanket from the backseat. He, however, brought none of the items that I remember him stuffing into the seats of the car. Perhaps that is to come later.

"The lady from the front counter stopped by and gave us a bunch of papers," my mother told him. "It says that dinner is in one hour. They seem to have set hours for each meal of the day, but we have to go down to the restaurant to eat. We can't bring it to the room."

"Okay," my father replied "That's good. I'm getting a bit hungry."

"Apparently, our sponsor will be covering the cost of our stay and all our food," she continued.

"Even better. That means we can save our money," he stated.

"We spent most of our money buying the three-day pass to get to Traiskirchen," she confessed and waited for my father's response. He was quiet for a moment and then shrugged and replied, "it could have cost us much more."

He sat down on the bed and breathed a sigh of relief as he took in the room. I walked up and sat next to him on the firm mattress. He instinctively wrapped his strong arms around me and gave me a big hug and a kiss on my head, just like I hoped he would.

"We should find a way to call your parents tomorrow and let them know we made it," he said and my mother nodded in agreement.

"How long are we staying here, Daddy?" I asked.

"I don't know, honey, but it will be home for a while," he replied and smiled. "Why don't we go outside and look around."

We changed our clothes to something warmer and went outside to walk around the property that we would call home for a while. The air was crisp and clean, faintly fragranced with pine. The sun was still out but hiding behind a pillow of white puffy clouds. We walked directly across the street toward the meadow held in by a U-shaped tree line but were stopped by a wire fence, which kept us from walking into a deep yet narrow stream. On the other side of this rocky stream was the meadow I had spotted from the car, with multicolored cows roaming freely in it. We walked down to the little bridge I had noticed earlier. It was old and made of wood that had been stained grey from the years of snow exposure, too. It had remnants of crimson paint here and there and only held two of us at a time. We started to cross but paused when my father noticed fish below. We peered down at the rocky streambed that pushed the deep passing water into the places it wanted. In the smoother and deeper sections of the clear water, we saw large fish swimming against the pushing current. They were dark and long, not like the ones my father and I fished in Yugoslavia. I admired their determination to keep from being dragged downstream or pushed upon the surround black rocks. After a few moments, my parents continued on and I followed. There was a small path worked into the tall, yellowing grass that we followed. It led us along the lines of dark-green pine trees into the large square meadow ahead. We only went into the meadow a short distance. Before we realized, it was going to be a messy walk. There were large cows everywhere and among them were piles of manure everywhere you looked. The smell was not as pungent at the Penzion because of the cool breeze that moved through it, but being this close suddenly filled our nostrils with the smell of fresh manure and was enough to make us stop in our tracks. It seemed as though no one maintained this meadow at all. There were at least thirty cows, and after that I stopped counting. The path we were on would disappear and reappear but seemed to cut across the meadow diagonally and into the forest on the other side. We stopped and turned around retracing our steps back to the road. We made our way to the sign on the other side of the street, that I saw when we first arrived; "Penzion Adamtal." My mother told me to stand in front of it so she could take a picture. As I got closer to it, I saw the words Ramsau underneath it, the white paint peeling from the indentations of each letter in the wood. I turned and smiled as she took her picture. After that, we followed the building at its length, admiring the flowers and trees that were fenced in front of the building for decoration, and pointing out the spots that needed tending to. By the time we were done, the chill had worsened, so we headed into the lobby and past the desk to the restaurant for our scheduled dinner.

We were greeted by a similar-looking, husky, blonde woman and then seated us in a red-cushioned booth by a window facing the parking lot where our car stood. The food they served was hardy and warm. It was tasty, but by then, I was too tired to identify the details of each morsel that entered my mouth or the features upon our server's face. Within minutes, I drifted off.

It took weeks for us to settle into our new routine. I had made a friend, or an acquaintance at the very least. Her name was Veruska. She was slightly bigger than me, with long black hair and dark menacing eyes. Her family had arrived a couple weeks after us and took over the first room past the staircase banister, just before ours. I never really saw her family. She supposedly had a younger brother and both of her parents. My mother told me that she did not care for her, but she was the only girl I knew there. Otherwise, the time was very lonesome.

Winter came quickly, and the thick white snow covered the greenery I got so used to seeing. I spent my time building snowmen and balls of snow resembling the chef's head on the inn's signage, and playing in the white mush usually with my mother but sometimes with Veruska. My father had befriended the owner of Adamtal, Mr. Whitman, whom I never had the opportunity to meet, but whose name was mentioned often. He was also the proud owner of the cows, pastures and surrounding forests that surrounded the place. Mr. Whitman employed my father for the winter, supplying firewood from his forest and tending to the trees. It wasn't much money, my father claimed, but every little bit helps. Every day, I would watch him and one other man cross the road to the little wooden bridge and take the now snowed over path along the trees, diagonally through the meadow and into the thick tree line beyond it. Sometimes, I would walk with him as far as the bridge and watch him walk the rest of the way on his own, then occupied my time by watching the fish swim against the current of the stream that was now frozen over in most of the stagnant places. On rare occasions, my mother would come along, bringing stale bread with her that we then fed to the fish. I never saw what my father actually did in that forest, but his schedule was like clockwork. He left at nine in the morning and returned just before dinner.

One such winter's day, I walked my father to his path, bid him good-bye, and watched him walk the rest of the path until the trees in the distance consumed him. I stared at the fish below wondering how long they would fight their battles of swimming against the cold current before they gave up and surrendered to the power of the rushing water. I wondered how long my parents, much like these fish, planned on staying here and fighting this battle they had chosen to fight. My thoughts were distracted by Veruska, who was calling me from a distance. She was wearing her heavy winter coat, which made her look wider than usual. I started walking toward her.

"Hurry up!" she yelled.

I sped up into a light jog until I was in front of her.

"Come on!" she said in a daring tone and ran past the building to the old barn-looking structure. We walked around the back to a small grey, wooden door. She opened it and went in. It looked like a shed. It was dark and cold and snow had dropped into the room from various openings in the walls and ceiling. I stood in the doorway hesitant to go in, but before I could argue, she pulled me in and closed the door behind me. To my relief, the door wouldn't close all the way and left a good four-inch gap, which allowed light to escape through as if there to lend me a hand.

"Look!" she said, as she pulled out a small box of matches. She tried to light one of the wooden sticks, but failed. She tried another; it lit up but went out just as quickly. "Hold this," she demanded, as she shoved a piece of white paper into my gloveless hands.

"Maybe we shouldn't be doing this," I objected meekly. She shot me an evil look that made me instantly swallow my words.

She lit another match. This one took and she moved it closer to me to light the paper I held in my hands. Before I could react, the paper shot up in tall orange flame and consumed my entire hand burning the skin around my thumb. I dropped the engulfed paper on the ground as fast as I could react, but the damage had been done. My hand throbbed, as I tried to stomp out the remaining flames so the place wouldn't catch fire. Veruska ran out of the shed laughing hysterically as if another person embodied her soul. When the fire was completely out and my heart stopped racing, I opened the door and tried to close it behind me as best as I could so that no one would know we had been there. Veruska was nowhere to be seen. I was kind of relieved actually, so I didn't try calling out her name to track her down. I picked up some fresh snow from the hillside and placed it on my burned hand. Why would she do that? What was the point? I felt guilty for going in the shed to begin with, but more than anything, I was trying to figure out what to say to my mother. I had to go see her, my hand was charred and red, and throbbing pain filled it. I began making my way to the front of the building and up the stairs that led to our room. Veruska had disappeared.

I opened the door and went in. My mother was seated at the table with her back toward me, a mirror in one hand and a makeup brush in the other.

"Mommy?" I carefully got her attention.

"What is it, Lucie?" she asked, as she put her mirror down to look at me. She must have read it in my face or seen the snow on my hand. "What happened?!" she yelled, dropping everything on the table in front of her and running toward me.

"Veruska took me to the barn and made me hold a piece of a paper and then she lit it on fire and… and…" and I started to cry. The shame and anger I felt were far worse than the current pain of my burned hand.

"Let me see," she grabbed my hand and walked me to the sink. She took a wet towel and began to carefully wipe the snow and dirt off the wound. She looked angry. She didn't say anything as she treated my wounds and wrapped my hand in the gauze from her medical kit, which she took everywhere. When she was satisfied with her work, she put everything away and started toward the door.

"Stay here," she demanded and left the room. I heard her knocking on Veruska's door and then proceed to yell at the person who answered. I couldn't distinguish what she was saying and I was too afraid to try and find out. A short while later, she returned. "You are not to see that girl again!" she proclaimed. I dared not argue.

I didn't see Veruska for several days following that event and didn't speak to her for some time even after that. My hand healed quickly except for two small spots right at the base of my right thumb. They were still red, and the skin looked different there. It stood up in that area and was very smooth. I nursed it every morning and every night with the cream my mother had taught me to apply. It didn't hurt as much anymore except when I ran my hands under hot water.

About a week later, I was making my way up the stairs to go to our room when Veruska appeared at the top of the staircase. The minute she saw me, her face turned cold. It was as if the devil had taken a hold of her. Her dark eyes narrowed, her thin lips turned to a snarl, and she lunged at me with her fingers like claws. She grabbed a hold of my neck and began to squeeze, choking me with a strength I was not prepared for. I fought as hard as I could to get her off of me. She was not that much bigger than me and yet she held on to my neck like a tiger hanging on to its prey. I couldn't get her off. The harder I fought, the more she squeezed. I began to lose my senses and panic set in. I started banging my hands and legs on the wall behind me until I lost my balance and fell to the wooden floor beneath me. I was only inches away from the first stair of the staircase when my vision started to get fuzzy. She was determined to kill me. I looked toward the door of our room in hope that someone would come out and save me. At first, there was nothing, and then the door opened. My mother's head poked out and my vision went dark. In sudden shock, I heard her scream my name. She had seen me. In an instant, she had Veruska by the hair and was pulling her off of me. I began to cough and massage my neck. As my senses returned and my vision cleared, I saw my mother vigorously beating Veruska. She hit her wherever her hands happened to land. I was afraid she was going to kill her, but had not the strength to stop her.

Moments later, as Veruska lay curled up in a ball on the floor, crying and my mother lashing her fury into her, screaming at her, the door to Veruska's room opened. A woman I presumed to be her mother stepped out and screamed. My mother stopped and looked at her. Within seconds, she abandoned Veruska and collected me with ease and haste. She stepped between Veruska and her mother and yelled at them at the top of her lungs, "Your daughter should be locked up. She is crazy! Almost killed my daughter, and I would have killed her in return without a second thought. Don't you teach your daughter any manners or discipline? If you know what is good for you, you won't dare show your faces again!" With a series of strides, she had me in the room, safe.

After gaining her composure back, she started inspecting my neck. Asking me to turn it every which way and asking if I had pain or problems swallowing. I obliged her in hopes that she would not be mad at me.

When she managed to return to her calm self, she asked me what happened.

"I don't know. I was just coming up the stairs and she lunged at me and started choking me," I managed to mutter, tears streaming down my face. To my surprise, my mother wrapped her arms around me, holding me close to her and she, too, began to cry.

"It's okay," she whispered, "you're okay."

I didn't see Veruska or her family again after that day.

15

Winter soon turned to spring, and the snows melted to reveal a light-green haze over every bit of brown earth. Flowers of pastel color and various lengths covered the meadows and hillsides. The stream had thawed, and smaller baby fish could be spotted swimming their way against the current alongside their parents. With spring came new families to the place, my father's job was no longer needed, and we were scheduled to make a trip back to Traiskirchen.

When we arrived, we were told that our sponsor would pay for our way to America. They gave my parents a small map and a selection of locations that were listed on the back of it and asked us where we wanted to go. My parents didn't have an answer. They were unfamiliar with all the names of locations and asked if they could talk about it and get back to them. They scheduled another meeting several weeks later.

Over the course of the next few days, the discussions were endless about which city to choose. My father had requested another job of the owner, telling him he wished to save up some money. Mr. Whitman had a son who was a racecar driver and owned a gas station a few miles away in a town called Heinfeld. My father accepted a job there and, from then on, was on a new routine of driving to Heinfeld three times a week to work at the gas station Mr. Whitman's son owned. Being so far, my father rarely made it back in time for the scheduled dinner hour, and my mother would sneak food into her pockets and purse and save it in the room for him to eat when he returned. I spent most of my time outside. There were now several children there I could play with, which made the time pass a little faster. I spent my time playing tag, picking flowers, and rolling down hills, just like every other child did. Only on one of these days, I rolled down a hill so hard the tall grass ripped out my dangling gold earring that I had had since birth. Search as I might, it was lost forever in the tall spring grass.

My father spent most of his free time during the spring taking apart the seats in the Saab and removing all the hidden clothing and pots and pans that he had stuffed there months before. They were all intact. My father brought them up in small increments as to not raise questions from anyone around.

When Easter came around, the Penzion had the Easter celebrations set up for all the children. They had supplied long branches from a weeping willow, various colors of ribbons, baskets, and bows. We each took three branches and braided them with ribbon into an Easter whip, as was tradition. Then we got dressed up and went door to door of the Penzion saying our rhyme to give us treats or its whipping time. Treats came in all sorts of forms there; it was whatever people could afford. Candy, chocolates and even decorated eggs were placed in our Easter baskets. It was a festive day for kids and adults and a nice change from the normal routine. I felt like a kid on that day, without worry or care.

Finally, the time came again to return to Traiskirchen and give them an answer. Only my father went this time, and my mother had told me they had picked this city called San Francisco. When I asked her why, she responded by saying it was the only city they recognized because they once heard it in a song. She also said that they had gotten a hold of the Rihas, and they were being sponsored by some of their friends in America to go to Oakland, CA, and that they thought it was nearby.

"Why do we have to go there, Mommy?" I asked, "Why can't we go home?"

It was a question I asked often, but never got a reply that satisfied me.

16

We spent several months there, nine to be exact. We watched families come and go, others came and stayed. Fall turned to winter, and winter turned to spring. When summer hit the land, we were transferred to a Penzion in Maria Schutz. I didn't know where this was, only that it was still in Austria and that it was where we were to go to learn about America before leaving Europe. My parents spent several days packing and rearranging all the added inventory that had lived in the seats of the car and then we were ready to go. Before leaving, I silently walked the property one last time, remembering my fire encounter, my near-death choking, Christmas, the Easter festivities and took the time to give one more go at finding my lost gold earring, which now I only sported one of. No luck. I wandered over to the little bridge that had become my ritual and watched the fish one last time. After a few moments, my father came to join me. Without saying a word, he took his place next to me and wrapped his arm around me.

"It's been quite a journey, hasn't it?" he asked me. I stood staring at the fish below unresponsive. "You know sometimes we do things to improve our lives. Your mother and I want to be in a place where we have opportunity and we can grow and make something of our lives. We want to make our lives better, make your life better," he paused. "I know that you may not understand much of this and I don't know if I'm explaining this very well, but we will do this together and your mother and I will always be there for you no matter what. Okay?"

I looked at him and nodded. He gave me a hug, and we stood in comfortable silence staring at the fish below. My mother approached us shortly after.

"Looks like the babies are growing up," she commented on the fish, not knowing the conversation that had just taken place.

After watching them swim and fight their daily battle, my father asked, "Shall we?" as he put his hand firmly on my shoulder and guided me away from the little bridge, my mother at his side. We walked to the car and got in. I looked upon the building and the property that had been my home for the last nine months, one last time as we drove away.

17

We arrived in Maria Schutz later that afternoon. It was another Penzion, though not nearly as big. It had one of the deepest and biggest ceramic bathtubs I had ever seen. We spent the first night there, taking turns soaking in the tub until the water turned our skin into pruny valleys. We were to spend a week here with daily classes as a type of orientation to the US culture. We learned basic English words, about holidays, and general information about the individual states and so on. It was all boring to me and I found myself losing consciousness on my mother's skinny arm during most of these classes.

During the day, my mother was pouring over large maps and reading the papers for all the incoming news. She was obsessed! An overseas PanAm flight had an unexplained malfunction and went down. There were no survivors. She was in a frantic disposition.

My father used this time to sell our faithful Saab 900, which held strong during our journey. I knew he was in a hurry to sell it as we were scheduled on a Pan Am flight later that same week, so he ended up selling it for a small amount of cash and a Sharp radio with a built-in tape player. It was not what he had hoped for, I know, because I heard all the commotion over it, but it was all he could get at that time.

With the decent-sized tan radio now in our room, my mother never turned it off. It either played music in languages I couldn't understand or spouted out the daily news. Two more Pan Am flights had crashed in the week, leading up to our departure. I overheard them describe the crashes over the radio.

"Maybe we should call this off," my father said "What if OUR plane crashes? Then what?"

My mother pleaded with him. "Think about how far we have come. It would be crazy to give up now. Besides, if we go back they could lock us up, lock our families up if they found out they knew of our escape. Can you imagine that?"

The conversations were intense and not pleasant to be around. I could tell there was risk, but I also trusted my parents. I had no other choice but to trust them. We made one final call to my mother's parents, letting them know we were scheduled on the PanAm flight to San Francisco via Hamburg and that our sponsor, AFCR (American Fund for Czechoslovak Refugees), would cover the cost of the flight and set us up with housing and a job once we got there. I said my good-byes to my grandparents, who were tearful on the other end of the line, but the time on the pay phone was almost up and my parents took over for the final exchange of words.

I didn't know how or what to feel. Scared? Sad? Angry? Excited? I was not as confused as before. I understood a little more of what was going on at this point, but I still didn't know if I wanted to be a part of it. Did I really have a choice anyway?

18

On June 24, 1985, we arrived by bus at the international airport in Vienna and boarded our PanAm flight to America via Hamburg. I sat between my parents and remember a fellow refugee taking a picture of me and my parents just before takeoff. There was tension in the air. Everyone on the plane was scared that this flight might go down, too, and their struggles to get this far would have been in vain. It was a tremendously long flight. I slept here and there, but my parents seemed to stay up the entire way. The small portal windows that were once bright with the sun turned star studded then dark before they turned to sun again. My parents and even the stewardess occupied my time with card games and memory games and coloring books all provided by PanAm. They served us hot meals that were actually quite tasty, but the movies and games fell short on my attention span and I was bored out of my mind for that many hours. My back and butt hurt from all the sitting, as walking and stretching was limited on the plane. It seemed like we were on the plane for days when we finally touched down in New York on June 25, 1985.

It was a stop no one told me about. We all got off the plane in New York and were processed as immigrants of Europe. They took pictures, fingerprints, and all the documentation we had been provided, giving us additional paperwork to fill out. We were to all sign them before they got returned. My mother signed my name for me, and then we were escorted to another flight. We arrived at the San Francisco International Airport just before midnight. We waited forever for our bags to come through the terminal. At around 1:00 a.m., the AFCR van pulled up, loaded up our things and drove us to our future home. I couldn't see much outside other than the lights of the streets and shops that lined the somewhat dirty road and the exhausted look on my parent's faces.

We pulled onto a street called Pierce St., and the van pulled to a stop and began unloading. We had arrived. As we stepped out of the white van, I looked around. We were in a somewhat deserted but well lit back parking lot that fenced in it and the building in front of us. The building was tall and dark with several levels. There was a metal staircase that led from the ground up to the roof, pausing at each level. My parents gathered our things, and a tall, thin woman escorted us into the building. There were people, dark but smelly silhouettes, sleeping on the ground as we passed by. We entered the building through the back door and walked up the stairs. They were cement stairs held up by iron railing. There were men on these stairs as well. They looked at us from the corners of their eyes as we passed by. We stopped climbing the stairs when we got to the second floor. She led us to the door marked #10 and unlocked it using her key. She entered the apartment, lit a couple tall wax candles so that we could see and then handed the keys to my mother, asked her to sign a piece of paper, and retreated back into the dark hallway, leaving us with only a few parting words and the emptiness and darkness of our new home. I scanned the room, for that is all it was, a large room. There was a small kitchen the length of the shortest wall to the left of the door. One large and one small space-themed mattress that lay in the middle of the floor with a pile of thin, blue blankets upon them and a large window that failingly decorated the wall behind it. There was one bathroom with a toilet, sink, and bathtub shower. This is what we left our beautiful home in Teplice for? My scan was interrupted by my mother's sarcastic laugh.

"There is champagne in the sink! And a note, 'Welcome to America,'" she read. "The ice seems to be melted so it's warm. There is no hot water, no electricity. What do we do?"

My father just looked at her and said, "Let's just get some rest. We will deal with the rest of this in the morning."

She shrugged and nodded in agreement. Before she could do anything else, there was a knock at the door. "Who could that be?" my mother asked, as my father headed for the door.

"Hey!" he exclaimed, happily greeting the person at the door. We all looked to see who he was so happy to see and in walked Zdenek Riha.

"Hi, guys! I got in a week ago and found out where you were staying. Wanted to give you a proper welcome to America," he said smiling.

"Oh my gosh, Zdenek!" my mother cried and they shared a hug. "I'm so glad you guys are okay. It's so nice of you to stop by…"

The words continued, but I was too tired to follow along. After all the formalities and discussions of our trip, my father decided to open the bottle of champagne.

"It's only right that we share this bottle. After all, we started this journey together and we made it! Seems only right we celebrate together," my father declared as he took the foil off the top of the bottle and began to unwind the wire holding the cork in place.

My mother prepared glasses, well white ceramic cups that were already in the shelves and even put one out for me. POP! Went the cork on the green and gold bottle.

"Oh no!" cried my father.

"Hurry over the sink!" cried my mother.

The champagne cork shot in the air along with most of the champagne. It flowed out of the bottle as if it were being pushed up from the bottom. It was everywhere, the countertops, floors, my father's hair, everywhere. They laughed it off and poured the remaining liquid into the cups. My mother handed me one and said, "Just this once."

"To the success of one journey and to the success of the next," my father cried as everyone raised their glasses. "Let's hope America gives us the opportunities and the lives we've been looking for."

"Here, here!" exclaimed my mother and Zdenek, as they toasted their cups and then bent down to toast mine. After the clink of the cups, I did as they did and raised the cup to my lips to drink. The liquid was warm and bubbly. It was sweet yet bitter. One sip was enough and I spit the remainder back in the cup. They all laughed, as they caught me wiping the remnants of the unpleasant flavor off my tongue.

"Here, let me have it," my mother said, taking the cup with the remaining liquid in it.

The celebration was over as quickly as it started. Not only was the liquid gone at this point, but Zdenek explained that he lived kind of far and had to start his drive back. He left my mother a number he could be reached at, along with an address. After saying his good-byes, he, too, disappeared into the dark hallway, leaving my mother and father wiping down the spilled champagne.

I started to doze off on one of the exposed mattresses. It was covered with images of space and invited me in to sleep, but had no sheets on it. I sat on the one that had the light-blue blankets and noticed a couple of smaller pillows behind them and served in supporting my heavy body in my slumped-over seated position.

My mother must have noticed me because, the next thing I knew, she was taking my shoes off, putting on my pajamas and settling me into the smaller of the two mattresses. I dozed in and out as the sounds of the street below were loud and would wake me periodically. There were no curtains on the tall window, and the yellow light from the street lamp shone right onto the wooden floor in front of me. A man shouted on the streets below and I was jerked awake. I looked around, but there was no one there. My parents were but two hilly silhouettes on the mattress at my feet. I readjusted my little pillow and lay back down, glancing at the stream of light in front of me before the weight of my eyelids forced my eyes shut. Something was off. I opened my eyes again. The floor was black except for the spot where the light hit. There it was brown. Yet the floor seemed to be moving. Maybe it was just my imagination. I adjusted my pillow again and settled in with eyes closed. Then I heard a sound like something scurrying across the floor. I opened my eyes again, this time searching the floor for the sound. It WAS moving... the floor was moving! I stared at it intently as I pulled the light blanket close to me as if it would protect me from whatever was out there. Then something big scurried in front of me right through the beam of light.

"Mom!" I screamed. "Mom!"

My mother sat straight up in bed, "What? What's going on?"

"There is something on the floor! It's moving! And something just scurried across the floor in front of me," I yelled.

"Okay, shhh..." she said, all groggy. "Joe, wake up, there is something on the floor." She nudged my father.

She reached over to where she had left the burned down candle from earlier in the night, relit it, and held it up high. The soft yellow light flooded the room and created a shimmer on the moving floor. It was brown and moving in clumps with tentacles everywhere!

"Oh my God!" she screamed flying to her feet.

"I told you!" I exclaimed.

My father got to his feet and lit the other candle. "Cockroaches! They must be after the champagne," he said.

Wherever the light from the candle hit, they scurried away from it as if it would kill them. Cockroaches, brown and several inches long, disappeared into the walls and under the cabinets as if being sucked from the floor. Several of them scurried across my blanket. I screamed again and sprung to my feet, wiping myself off as if they were crawling all over me. I jumped onto the warm mattress my parents had only moments ago abandoned.

"What do we do?!" my mother cried.

"We can leave the candles burning so they don't come near us?" my father suggested. It was the only option they could come up with this late at night.

I slept in their bed that night, paranoid at every sound. *Welcome to America*, I thought. By daybreak, my mind was exhausted and I fell asleep.

19

The tall, thin lady that let us into our apartment came back for us in the same AFCR van from the night before. She took us into the city into a tall building with the letters INS written on the side. We stood in line with several other immigrants who had arrived. They had processed our paperwork from the day before, we answered some other questions, and they handed us small laminated cards that read Alien Registration in big bold letters across the top and features our pictures and signatures. Then they processed us for a thing called social security. After hours in this building, we were taken into a room with other immigrants, where my parents quickly made acquaintances and jotted down names and numbers as references. By the end of the day, the apartment that was to be our home had hot water and electricity. They also provided us with sheets and basic essentials for our living needs. Our other personal items had not arrived yet and wouldn't for another couple weeks, as they were going by boat.

It didn't take long for us to realize that we were not in the best part of town. AFCR had put on a meet and greet party for all immigrants to attend where my parents would meet others like them, and issued my parents $25 a person per week for living expenses as well as food stamps. They set up English classes two to three times a week for three months and then they were to be placed in jobs.

My parents spent their time discussing the situation and wondering if they had done the right thing. They had exchanged the money that my father had made in Austria and the money left over from their escape. It totaled 2,500 in US currency. They decided that they needed a car, so my father went out looking. He didn't speak the language, but seemed to be determined. After being gone all day, he came home with a station wagon. It was beige, the tires were old, and the front windshield was missing and only held a few shards of remaining glass. There were large dents almost everywhere you looked, the rear bumper was missing, the air conditioner wasn't working, the leather seats inside were torn up, and the exhaust was dragging on the ground. It had the words Chevy Malibu on the back of the dented trunk that was forced shut. "It was the best I could do" my father said, "I will fix her up over time. I know she is not much to look, at but, most importantly, she runs and only cost a reasonable portion of what we have."

He kept his word, too, over the next three months. My father fixed up the windshield so that the car was secure, jimmy rigged the exhaust so it wouldn't drag, and, with the help of some other immigrants he had met, got it to look fairly decent. He also realized that we wouldn't last long on the mere food stamps and $75 a week we were getting.

In those three months, the rest of our belongings arrived, my parents had made some friends, and my father found work in a city called Belmont. Soon, we were moving again. This time, the building was big and super clean. It had a wide staircase that led to our apartment on the second floor and no men sleeping on its cement steps. It was a nice apartment and much bigger than the one we were in. Heck, anything was better than the cockroach- and ant-infested apartment we were in. Mom's new friend Liba helped her find it and get settled in. There were consequences to this move that my parents were not at first aware of. I found my mother crying one afternoon. She tried to hide it but failed. Later that day, I heard her talking to my father.

"They won't give me any more food stamps or our weekly allowance because we moved out of the area that they supervise. They also somehow found out that you have a job now. They are taking away the English classes and everything! They say we are on our own," she cried.

My father sat there comforting her the best way he knew how while absorbing this information. Liba's husband Ivan owned a garage called Marko Garage in a city called San Mateo and he decided to employ my father as a mechanic there, unofficially, of course. How they came to find out was a mystery to her.

"It's going to be okay," he said, "I can make the money. We will be okay. We just have to work together."

20

Liba and Ivan had two sons, Tom and David. Tom, who was tall for his age with freckles and blond spiky hair, ended up in first grade with me that fall. I was terrified. I didn't speak English and I barely knew Tomas, but he was kind enough to walk me to my class. I didn't understand a word anyone said to me, which frustrated me on a daily basis and caused me to speak less and less. On most days, I came home crying. I wanted to go home. My mother was at her wit's end and found nothing left to do or say but cry with me. My father was the only one who remained strong. He showed no defeat and no tears. He was determined and always managed to produce a positive outcome, whether money, furniture, or clothes. I admired him for that.

After a few weeks, I became accustomed to going to school and copying the actions of the other students. I had a music class that I found to be my only happiness. The teacher was very pretty, short but slim with curly black hair and cherry red lips. She always wore a silk scarf of varying colors that was tied in a loose bow around her neck. She made me feel at ease. I would spend hours staring at her lips trying to make out the words that escaped them. I had no idea what I was singing, but it felt good to be part of something so expressive. I had always loved to sing but hadn't attempted it since we left Teplice. I had had nothing to sing about.

Liba would often come over and help me with homework or forms that I had brought home from school that neither my mother nor I could make heads or tails of. I experienced my first Halloween, thanks to her. She explained the holiday and what it was all about. So, this Halloween, my mother picked out a fancy blouse and matching flowing skirt that she had and decorated my face with makeup, put some pretty jewelry on me and curled my short golden hair, well, cleaned up the curls as I had plenty to go around. We arrived at Liba's house and they finished me off with a cardboard crown that was painted gold and a delicate, gold and white handkerchief that they used as a veil and had stapled to the back of the crown. I was a princess that Halloween. We went door to door, collecting candy in our pillowcases for hours. I had more fun looking at all the decorations and all the costumes than anything else. I didn't have to be me on this day. I didn't have to speak English or any other language. I was a princess from a faraway land and all I had to do was knock on a door and say, "Trick or treat." It became my favorite holiday and it was over way too fast.

There were only a few more weeks of school before the holidays, and my music class was putting on a show. I was in the choir, though I still had no idea what I was singing. They made us dress in Christmas colors and stand on dark-blue-carpeted risers in front of an entire audience. I was frozen with fear. What if someone notices that I don't know what I'm singing? Then the music started. My teacher took her place in front of us and I became fixated upon her cherry-red lips. I read every word that escaped them and mimicked the action she made. By the second song, I got enough courage to start singing the words I was trying to form, however timid they may have sounded. I got through it and was greeted with applause and smiles and then later by hugs and pride from my parents and Liba. I felt a sense of accomplishment, however out of place it was.

Christmas came quickly, and, even though my parents had little money, they still managed to put up a small tabletop tree. It was no bigger than the rabbit I held dear, with only a few decorations hanging from its feeble branches. My mother had put herself together, makeup, hair, and all, and cooked a delicious, yet nontraditional, Christmas dinner. Santa had even left me a little something under the tree, but I somehow knew deep down that it was a gift my parents had placed there. I was no fool to Santa Claus. As much as my parents wanted me to believe, there was a Christmas in Teplice that I caught my father placing presents under the tree. I put the clues together back then, but I let them believe that I had no idea, as I didn't want to ruin the smiles and joy on their faces. This year was no different. I got a puzzle box with two kittens wearing hats. I loved the picture and couldn't wait to put it together. It was a small gift, but I knew they worked hard to get it, and I loved them for it.

Just following Christmas, my parents took me on a road trip to visit the Rihas. They were somewhere in a place called Orange County. It took several hours to get there, and boy was I happy when we did, even though I had slept though most of it. They were staying with friends on the pretty street we pulled up on. It was lined with pink and white flowering trees and the sun was running its many rays through the branches so beautifully it made it look like a painting in motion. I stood there admiring it until I was shaken to reality by the calling of my name. I turned and found that my parents were already at the front door meeting the Rihas, and I was standing on the sidewalk by the car alone. I walked to them and entered the house.

21

It was a small, but quaint, house. There was a living room, dining room, and kitchen, which all seemed to melt into one, and somewhere in the back, I assumed, were the bedrooms. We had just arrived for lunch, which was already spread out on the glass table and everyone was gathered around it—Elena, Zdenek Jr., Klara, and a couple people I did not know. I ran to them!

"Hi, Zdenek! Hi, Klara!" I had not realized I would get to see them, and I had not seen them since our last encounter at Traiskirchen. We quickly exchanged hugs and settled down to eat. It was odd from then on out, as if we didn't know what to say to each other. Maybe there was nothing to be said at all.

After lunch, Zdenek, my father, and the tall man I didn't know got up and headed out the door.

"Where are they going?" I asked my mother.

"They are going to a town a little ways from here to look around," she explained. "There may be a possible job offer there for your father." She turned her attention back to walking the men out the front door.

I watched as the three men got into one of the other smaller cars parked on the street and drove away, smiling and talking. I went back inside the house to find everyone clearing off the white dishes and the remnants of lunch. Zdenek Jr. came running up to me.

"Are you excited?" he asked.

"Excited? Excited about what?" I replied.

"They are taking us to the beach!" he exclaimed. My face immediately lit up.

The beach! How exciting. It had been several months since I had seen the water. It was still a bit chilly to be in the water I thought, but I never pass up a chance to stick my toes in the sand and watch the sun play on the water. I ran to my mother accepting the new information.

"Are we going, too?" I asked her.

"Going where?" my mother asked.

"Zdenek said they are going to the beach. Are we going, too?" I asked again, this time a little more timid as I was afraid the answer would suddenly be no.

"Ellen, are you guys going to the beach?" she turned her attention to Elena.

"I thought it would be something to do. I was told about this beach that has rides along the shore and is really nice, so I thought Marie could take us there," she responded indicating to the woman whose house we were in.

"Can we go?" I asked again, full of anticipation.

"I guess," she responded.

Yes! The beach! I could barely contain myself. I ran to Zdenek Jr. "We are going, too!" I exclaimed.

Within an hour, although it felt a lot longer, all piled in Marie's car, which managed to hold all seven of us, we were headed down the road to where ever this beach was. The road we were on mesmerized me. It was wide and had many lanes all going in the same direction. I never knew so many cars existed.

It had been a while since we had left the quaint little house. We seemed to be moving really slowly to our destination and my butt was starting to cramp from sitting on my mom's lap in the backseat. I couldn't wait to get there, and this trip was not making my anticipation any easier. About a half hour later, we had arrived. The beach was filled with people! Some were in the water, some were walking along a cement walkway, while others were plopped on the sandy beach. It took a while to find a parking spot, and it seemed like everyone was trying to be helpful in pointing some out. I guess I wasn't the only one anxious to get out of the car. Marie finally parked the car along a nearby sidewalk, and we all piled out. My mother handed me a towel and I watched as Elena did the same to Zdenek and Klara, and then the three women proceeded to unpack a bunch of linen bags from the trunk. It was a nice, warm day out, but a constant chilly breeze hit our bodies as we stood there. "Wait for us," my mother said. "We are all going to walk down together." More waiting...oh the anticipation. Let's go already!

They finally coordinated all their bags and locked the car. We walked down the cement pathway toward the sandy beach. Zdenek, Klara, and I were all several steps ahead, anxious to drop our towels somewhere and hit the water, but our mothers kept hollering at us to slow down. When we finally reached the sand, we all instinctively removed our shoes and ran through it. It was almost yellow in color and coarse. The sand in Yugoslavia was almost white and smooth as could be. I inspected the sand closer and found tiny remnants of shell and coral. It was like pumice on my feet, but I didn't care. As we walked closer to the water and away from the protection of the palm trees, the sand began to get hotter and hotter. We started to make a dash for the water in hopes of cooling our feet. Within seconds, we were on the wet sand, and the water was playing with us by running away as we approached. Then when we got even closer to it, the water played with us again and rushed past our feet. We screamed. It was ice cold! How could anyone be in the water? We ran from it. It became a momentary game of playing tag with the water. There were little bubbles and ripples that formed in the sand as the water receded. After a while of observing this, my curiosity got the best of me and I knelt down for a closer look. Zdenek and Klara saw me and ran to help investigate my new discovery. The ripples were there only for a moment before disappearing again. Zdenek was the first to act, and he grabbed a handful of the sand. He started spreading it out in the palm of his hand as Klara and I watched closely. Within seconds, tiny little crabs revealed themselves. They were bluish grey, and the minute Zdenek exposed their hidden shells, they snapped at him. He dropped the sand, so he wouldn't get pinched. We all laughed as he ran to wash his hands in the nearest wave. Then we saw our mothers settling into a spot, and we all grabbed our towels and delivered them to their location. They detained us for a bit as they lathered sunscreen on our white bodies. I took the time to soak in the scenery.

There were men in the water, way out in the distance. They wore black skin like that of a seal and sat on long thin boards of some kind. When a wave formed, they would paddle to the very top of it and stand on their boards to ride the wave before it disappeared into the calm in front of it. I watched them with great amazement as they conquered one wave after the other. The waves were amazing here. They were large and strong and crashed with a power so intense it created foam at the shore. I had never experienced waves like these.

To my right was a pier surrounded by massive black rocks. Men were piled on the rocks and the safety of the pier in rows holding fishing rods and staring into the water like my father and I had done. At the very end of the pier was a building where people were coming in and out of in a steady stream.

To my left was a small playground that was almost deserted except for a handful of children half my size and the parents that watched them like hawks from the benches around it. It had swings, jungle gyms, a merry-go-round and a couple rides you put coins in. This must have been the "rides" that Elena had mentioned earlier. Beyond it, the beach continued as far as I could see with colorful buildings and a cement walkway lining its end.

The beach was littered with colorful towels and umbrellas. People lying out to absorb the sun and the heat of the sand that was now penetrating through the towel I was sitting on and warming my legs. It was such a different experience, yet just as soothing.

We spent several hours there. Playing with the little crabs in the coarse yellow sand, collecting colorful seashells that we proudly showed to our mothers, we played tag with the icy water until it won, built sand castles, buried each other in the sand, and then spent most of the time turning blue as we jumped in and out of the incoming waves. Our mothers beckoned us out of the water many times to warm our bodies, but we pretended not to hear them as we continued our adventures. Blue with cold, teeth chattering, there was nothing that could ruin our fun.

The day ended as quickly as it came, and, before we knew it, the sun was setting and we headed back to the house we had abandoned earlier that day. As we entered the house, we were surprised by the busy conversations of our fathers. They had returned and were drinking beer and talking loudly at the dining room table. I ran to my father and told him as much as I could about my adventures by the beach before my mother pulled me away. She was always cleaning me up, and this moment was no different. She was walking me to the bathroom to wash off the salt and sand from my body and hair.

When I returned, only my father was seated at the tall glass table, and sounds were coming from the back of the house. He sat quietly sipping on his glass of foaming yellow beer. I sat at the table next to my father, and he handed me a sandwich from the platter in the middle of the table. I accepted it and realized that I had been too busy playing to eat. Hunger was definitely starting to call to me.

"How did it go?" my mother asked my father.

"It went great. It is all settled. Zdenek and I start after the second week of January," he answered.

"That is in three weeks" she said surprised. "How was the town? Did you look at possible places to live?"

"Yeah, we looked around a bit. The town is small and very green. People seem nice. Reminds me of Europe a little," he said. "Zdenek is going to stay here so that he can start looking for a place now and get to know the town a little more. We are going to stay with them when we come back down and then he is going to take us around, I think you will like it."

"He thinks he's going to find a place that quickly?" she asked.

"Three weeks is a long time. I don't see why he wouldn't," he replied.

Zdenek and Elena returned to the dining room and sat down next to my parents, with Zdenek Jr. and Klara close behind. The evening was a celebration of drinking and eating. Everyone was happy, smiling, and in great spirits. It had been a long time since I had seen those bright smiles on my parents' faces and it put me in a good mood. We were moving again, but this time, into the same town as the Rihas and I could reunite with my friends again, and that made me happy.

We returned to Belmont the next day, and my parents began the process of yet again packing up all our belongings. We celebrated New Year with Liba and Ivan at their spacious, one-story house. It was happy yet sad. Liba had done so much for us and without Ivan, this move would not have been financially possible. It was a bittersweet celebration of good-byes and new beginnings.

22

On January 3, 1986, we arrived in Fallbrook. It was dark when we arrived, so there was little to see through my window. We stayed with the Rihas that night, as was planned, in an apartment they had found near one of the schools. We were exhausted and retired to our beds early that night, anxious for the next day's activities of establishing our new life.

The next morning, we drove around the town looking for our future home. Zdenek had already lived there two weeks and had gotten to know the place a little, so he took us to all the places he knew. We looked at several apartment complexes and found one that my mother took a fancy to. Alvarado Apartments. They were cream stucco buildings, with dark-brown wooden patios and accents, which sat on top of a tall hill. There was a large playground on the premises that would serve as my future entertainment.

My parents were shown an apartment on the second floor of the first building. The buildings had four apartments each, two on the bottom and two on the top, with an exterior staircase leading to the top-level units. The apartment was fairly large. It opened into a large living room on the right that emptied onto a small, enclosed balcony, a decent dining space, and a kitchen on the left and a hall straight down the middle that led to two bedrooms. The smaller bedroom was the first door on the right, and there was a full bathroom on the left. The hall ended with a white door to an oversized master bedroom. This room felt like it was two rooms sitting side by side. When you entered, there was a master bath on the left and a closet with mirrored doors straight ahead. To the right was a whole other room, one step up from the room I was in and ended with a large window that overlooked the driveway. My parents filled out the application for this apartment and answered the manager's questions as best as they could.

While we waited for the answer on the apartment, Zdenek took us over to the elementary school that Zdenek Jr, Klara and I were to attend. I was technically still on Christmas break, but school would start up again soon and my parents had to fill out the transfer papers to get me in. We pulled up to the school that was only four long blocks away from the apartments we had just found. It had a big sign out front with a white teddy bear wearing a red bow that read Maie Ellis Elementary.

We entered the admissions office, which was right in front of a back office to a room that read Principal. It had a tall counter I couldn't see over, lots of shaded windows and a rocking chair to the left of the door. In the rocking chair sat a stuffed white bear with a big red ribbon around his neck just like the one pictured on the sign out front. I walked up to it and was compelled to touch its fur. He was extra soft and the cutest bear I had ever seen, he was bigger than me by only a few inches. I sat down in the polished wood bench next to the rocking chair and rested my hand on the arm of the bear as if he were transferring courage to me in this moment of nervous tension.

Zdenek did most of the talking with my parents interjecting wherever they felt more explanation was needed. The lady at the counter could tell we didn't speak English and was doing her best to understand. She kept glancing over at me and smiling. After what seemed like an eternity of waiting, my parents had filled out the proper paperwork, and we were leaving the office. The kind lady stopped me at the door and handed me a red lollypop with a massive smile. She had a kind face and a calming energy. I smiled back and accepted her offering.

The town was supposedly small, but still felt big to me. It was very green and there was a town center that housed two grocery stores, a hardware store, a post office and some small boutiques. One section of town had a street that was full of really old looking western buildings. That street was about two blocks long and had these western buildings on either side of it. They were occupied by boutiques, ice-cream parlors and at the end of the second block was an old theater. It was a neat place and felt like something out of a storybook.

We spent the next couple days driving around and getting to know the area a little bit. We drove by my father's new job. It was on a street directly behind one of the grocery stores and looked like it was part of several buildings all bundled together. There was a refuse place, a machine shop, and a blacksmith. This is where my father and Zdenek would be working as blacksmiths. It struck me as odd. My father was a pilot back home, and he had worked in the forest, at a gas station, as a mechanic and now as a blacksmith. Where did he learn to do all these things? It was a thought I pondered over and over. I asked him one day and he responded by saying, "You learn. I have to make money." When that didn't resonate with me, he continued, "You can do anything you want if you put your mind to it and not fear it." These were words I would never forget.

On January 5, we moved into our new apartment. My parents surprised me and gave me the master bedroom. It was the very first time that I had had a room by myself. They said that it would give me room to play and have friends over and that in years to come I would have more stuff to fill the room then they ever would. I didn't know what they meant by that. My mother helped me arrange my mattress on the floor by the window. I put all my toys near my bed and then she helped me put all my clothes away in my very own closet. The space that was between the bathroom and the bed was large and empty. A whole other room would have fit in there. I felt like a princess. My very own room!

23

The next day, I started school. My parents drove me to school and walked me into the admissions office. That same kind-faced woman smiled and greeted us as we came in. She exchanged a few words with my parents and then smiled and took me by the hand. I looked to my parents for guidance but they motioned approvingly to go with her, so I did. The heels of her shoes clinked against the white concrete and echoed as she walked me down the corridor about five doors down from the admissions office and opened the tall white door to the right. She walked me in as I took one final glance at my parents, who were still standing at the door of the admissions office watching me.

The room was full of color and other children. I was obviously late. I didn't know where to look first. The walls were extra tall, and the ceiling was really high. There were windows but not the kind you could see out of. Most of them were near the ceiling, spilling light onto the tables and walls. On the walls hung letters, numbers, colors, and pictures, except for a section at the front of the room that had a long, green chalkboard. The room was covered in long tables that had been put together to form rows, and several children were seated at each table. They all looked at me as I entered. A thin, not so tall woman walked briskly toward me from the front of the room. She was a pretty lady, her pale blonde, almost spiky hair set with hairspray and her makeup perfectly done to accentuate her eyes and cheekbones. She smiled as she approached me, exposing her pearly whites. The two women exchanged words and paperwork.

"Mrs. Wurtz, this is Lucie," she said, introducing me to the teacher. "Lucie, this is Mrs. Wurtz." she continued, as she indicated to the lady by touching her hand. Mrs. Wurtz extended her hand to me to shake it, and I understood that this was an introduction. I politely took her hand and shook it. "She is an ESL student, so you will have to be patient with her. I have made arrangements for a tutor starting tomorrow," the kind faced woman explained and then turned to leave.

Mrs. Wurtz escorted me to a seat nearest her desk, all the while the class following me with their eyes and chatting, and then placed a hardback book in front of me along with a pencil. She smiled and then returned to the front of the room. I felt everyone's eyes on me staring and giggling. Mrs. Wurtz quickly regained their attention with calm poise. Today was writing. She instructed the children to open their hardback workbooks. They did so and I copied. I copied everything everyone else did for the rest of the day. There was one recess break and I spent it on the swings that sat in a large sandbox, not really swinging, just mulling over my past and future. The rest of the day finish in much the same manner as it started and came to an early end. My parents were again waiting by the admissions office and I followed them to the car.

"How was it?" my mother asked.

I shrugged as I got in the car.

"Did you understand anything going on?" she asked

"I just copied everything everyone else did," I answered.

She dropped the subject from then on out.

Dad was starting his job and needed the car, so I was forced to learn to take the bus, where I usually sat in the back by myself. The school had provided me a tutor that pulled me out of class every day for a couple hours and worked with me one on one, teaching me words and phrases and then returning me to my class. It helped. Everyone at the school was very kind to me, and I felt that they were trying to help. The kids weren't so bad either. After a couple days I learned that Klara was in second grade and Zdenek Jr. was in my same grade but had a different teacher. We saw each other at recess on occasion and that helped distract me from the feeling of alienation.

Over time, I did make a friend. There was a girl who lived in the same building as me but downstairs and to the right. Her name was Christina Marston. She was my same height with straight blonde hair past her waist that she always wore in a thick braid down her back. She had a younger brother and both parents. Her mother was a heavy smoker, so we spent most of our time outside, but she was the only person who didn't care that I didn't understand everything. She took the time to teach me, even if she didn't realize she was doing so.

I picked up the language enough to sufficiently communicate within a year, which boosted my confidence to make friends, although my friends tended to be the ones who lived in my apartment complex or were in my class. Zdenek and Klara developed other interests, and the three of us remained friends but saw each other less often. I remained fairly shy and didn't seek out many friends or activities. My mother remained at home and did the cooking and took care of anything and everything she could. It was a job she held that we all took for granted and rarely recognized verbally. My father quit his job at the blacksmiths a few months later after discovering that Zdenek had been pocketing a portion of his paycheck. He got a temporary job as a mechanic in a neighboring city until he was hired by a local garage permanently. My parents both scrapped and saved every penny they earned and continued to upgrade our living situation. It started with actual beds and then shelving and couches and so on. We moved again a few short years later to a brand new apartment complex near the center of town. We were the first tenants in the building. My mother was taking English classes and was proficient enough to speak to the owner, who took a liking to her and offered her a job as the complex manager, lowering our rent by half. She accepted and convinced the Marstons to move as well so that my now best friend Christina and I could remain in contact. They became the second tenants in the complex. The apartments had two bedrooms, one bath with large windows. I still had my own room though not nearly as large as the one I had. Our dining room overlooked a pool, which I spent the majority of my free time in. My mother utilized my English skills to deal with problem tenants, even though I was only nine and hardly put fear into the hearts of people in the building. We didn't stay in this apartment long, maybe two years before my parents had saved enough to buy land and build a house on the outskirts of town about 15 minutes away. Although this had a cost, as Christina's family didn't like driving so far and that seemed to be the consensus of most friends' parents.

From nothing to a house and land. The property was on top of a large, sunny hill. Two and a half acres of dark-green avocado trees, although we had no experience with the fruit at all and disliked the taste at first. My parents had built a spacious three-bedroom, two-bath Spanish style home on the highest point of the hill. I had few friends to come visit, but found my time occupied by helping cut trees, harvest fruit, and tend to and improve the property at my parents' side. Eventually, I would be working with my father in his very own garage in the center of town as the primary English speaker. It was the beginning of a whole new journey, and my life still had yet to begin.

About the Author

Lucie Grimm was born and raised in former Czechoslovakia. In 1984 her family immigrated to the United States of America to avoid the Communist invasion of that period. This book is a tell all of that journey to the United States as remembered and interpreted by a six year old girl. The United States was a cultural shock but in time grew to be a blessing in her life. In her early teens, Lucie found acceptance in the world of theatre as a singer and actor, while working for her father in their local car repair and restoration shop in Southern California. With many mentors and positive influences in her life, she pursued a successful climb in musical theater while learning the foundations of good business and hard work. Despite the invaluable training she received in the family business, performing became her passion and obsession. Lucie has performed in numerous stage shows, tours and even international productions as a singer, actress, dancer and spokes model. She even appeared in several TV and Film productions including James Cameron's blockbuster film Titanic.

Today, Lucie is the right-hand lady to husband singer/songwriter Michael Grimm, while still giving herself plenty of time pursuing her own artistic release while settling into a whole new way of life.

For more on Lucie Grimm, visit: www.luciegrimm.com

www.ingramcontent.com/pod-product-compliance
Lightning Source LLC
Chambersburg PA
CBHW060333260626
47160CB00007B/2787